Praise For
THE BLUESUIT CHRONICLES

"The first installment of The Bluesuit Chronicles, (*The War Comes Home*) is a compelling start to what is sure to be an epic saga. A former Golden Gloves boxer and Army medic returns home from Vietnam to a very different America than the one he left. The drug craze of the early seventies takes a heavy toll on the Boomer generation, and the social fabric begins to unravel, nail-biting action, romance, and intrigue, based on actual events." Rated Four Stars.
~ Red City Reviews

"From the moment I started reading *The War Comes Home*, I couldn't put it down. I was captivated by the balance of action and drama that John Hansen expertly weaves throughout this fast-paced historical fiction. I'm looking forward to reading the next one."
~ S. McDonald, Redmond, WA

"An exciting, read, riveting action, romance and moving scenes. *The War Comes Home* took me back to the Bellevue I knew in 'the good old days.' Impossible to put down." ~ Cynthia Davis, Bellevue, WA

"*The War Comes Home* follows the activities of two city police officers, Hitchcock and Walker, as they prepare and then head out for the nightly patrol of their neighborhood streets. Hitchcock feels a strange foreboding that there will be danger that evening, and someone will die. The two police officers spend the evening patrolling areas looking for drug dealers, prostitutes, and other criminals.

This manuscript is extremely well-written. The author has infused the prose with an interesting mix of dialogue, inner thoughts. The characters are nicely developed, the dialogue is genuine and flows organically. The reader is immediately drawn into the story and wants to learn more, not only about the officers, but what awaits them as they begin their nightly patrol." ~ Review by an editor at Bookbaby

John Hansen
July 2021

Praise For
THE BLUESUIT CHRONICLES

"Having grown up in Bellevue in the '60s and '70s, I bought the entire series for my husband for his birthday. He is completely engrossed in them. Thank you, John, for writing them. It's hard to get him to relax, and the books are doing it with laughter and 'do you remember' comments. We are eagerly waiting for the next book to come out."
~ Jeanie Hack, Bellevue, WA

"Book Two of The Bluesuit Chronicles series, *The New Darkness*, continues the story of Vietnam veteran Roger Hitchcock, now a police officer in Bellevue, Washington. The spreading new drug culture is taking a heavy toll on Hitchcock's generation. Some die, some are permanently impaired, everyone is impacted by this wave of evil that even turns traditional values inside out. Like other officers, the times test Hitchcock: will he resign in disgust, become hardened and bitter, corrupt, or will his background in competition boxing and military combat experience enable him to rise to meet the challenge? Romance, intrigue and action are the fabric of *The New Darkness*."
~ Amazon.com

"*Valley of Long Shadows* is the third book in The Bluesuit Chronicles... Returning Vietnam veterans who become police officers find themselves holding the line against societal anarchy. Even traditional roles between cops and robbers in police work have become more deadly... The backdrop is one of government betrayal, societal breakdown, and an angry disillusioned public. The '70s is the decade that brought America where it is now.
Four Stars Rating ~ Red City Reviews

"Received Book 4, *Day Shift* on a Wednesday. Already done reading it. Couldn't help myself. Was only going to read a couple chapters and save the rest for my upcoming camping trip. LOL. 3 hours later book finished. Love it. 2 Thumbs up!!! ~ Alanda Bailey, Kalispell, MT

Praise For
THE BLUESUIT CHRONICLES

"By the time I finished reading the series up through Book Four (*Day Shift*), I concluded most men would like to be Hitchcock, at least in some way. What sets him apart is the dichotomy of his makeup: he grew up with a Boy Scout sense of honor and right and wrong, yet he isn't hardened or jaded by the evil and cruelty he saw when he went to war, though he killed in combat. As a policeman he *chooses* good and right: to do otherwise is unthinkable. He is a skilled fighter, yet so modest that he doesn't know he is a role model for others around him, and women feel safe with him. I know Hitchcock's type—two of my relatives were cops who influenced my life:"
~ Tracy Smith, Newcastle, WA

"Book Five (*Unfinished Business*) moves to show how difficult it is for Officer Hitchcock to do right. Bad people are out to get him for his good work. He is a threat to their nefarious activities. There is even a very bad high-ranking policeman who puts Hitchcock and his family in extreme peril. Organized foreign crime is moving into his city, he works hard to uncover the clues to solve this evil in his city. I'm still waiting to find out what restaurant owner Juju is up to and who she works for. Great series and story. Another fine book by John Hansen. Yo! ~ T.A. Smith

"I've read all of John's books and rated them all 5 stars, because those stars are earned. I worked the street with John as a police officer for years and what he speaks of in his books is real. John is an excellent author; articulate and clear, always bringing the reader directly into the story. I like John's work to the point that I've asked him to send me any new books he writes; I'll be either the first or almost the first to read all of them. I lived this with John. He's an author not to be missed. You can't go wrong reading his books. I strongly encourage more in the series." ~ Bill Cooper, Chief of Police (ret)

Praise For
THE BLUESUIT CHRONICLES

"John Hansen has written another great read. *Unfinished Business* is filled with conspiracy, corruption and crime, much of which is targeted at Hitchcock. From the beginning of the book, I was hooked. The author has a gift with words that drew me into the story effortlessly— I could not put the book down. I have read all in the series and I look forward to reading more of John Hansen's books." ~ S. McDonald

"A viewpoint from the inside: I worked with and partnered with John both in uniform and in detectives, and like him I came to the Department after military service. This is the fifth (as of this date) of five books in this series. I have read and re-read all five books, and for the first time, recently, over a two-day period, read the entire series in order. All five books were inspired by John's experiences, during many of which I was present. John is an extremely gifted author and I was transported back to those times and experienced a full gamut of emotions, mostly good, sometimes less so. His use of humor, love, anger, fear, camaraderie, loyalty, respect, disapproval, devotion, and other emotions, rang true throughout the books." ~ Robert Littlejohn

"The whole series of The Bluesuit Chronicles brought back a flood of memories. I started in police work in 1976. This series starts a couple of years earlier. The descriptions of the equipment, the way you had to solve crimes without the assistance of modern items. John made me feel that I was there when it was happening. This whole series is what police work is about. Working with citizens, caring about them, and catching the bad guys. Officers in that time period cared about what they did. It wasn't all about a paycheck... We were the originators of community policing. We knew our beat and the people in it. I am not saying we were perfect; however, we were very committed to our community. That being said, I can't wait for the next book. Please read the whole series. Once you start you won't stop."
~ Garry C. Dixon, Ret. LEO-Virginia

Praise For
THE BLUESUIT CHRONICLES

"Retired Detective John Hansen is a master writer. He brings to life policing in the Northwestern U.S. during the '70s; a transitional period. One has to wonder of how much of his writings are founded in personal experience vs. creative thinking. Either way, his stories are thoroughly enjoyable and well-worth purchasing his original books in this series, his current release, as well as the books yet to come."
~ Debbie M.-Scottsdale, AZ

"I urge you to complete your 'to do' list prior to reading *Unfinished Business*, as once started, I could not put it down. It was always, 'one more page' and soon I was not getting anything else done, but it was well worth it. The author has an amazing way of drawing the reader into each scene, adding to the excitement, sweet romance, raw emotion and revealing of each fascinating character as the plots unfold. I highly recommend this book to anyone who wants a truly good read. Looking forward to the next book from this highly talented author." ~ Cynthia R.

"I received the 5th book in The Bluesuit Chronicles and started reading and per usual, didn't stop until I finished the book. I am a huge fan of John's stories. I grew up in the general area that the stories are set in. Also, in the same time frame. John's books are always fast paced and entertaining reads. I would recommend them to any and all."
~ A. Bailey-Kalispell, MT

Also by John Hansen:

The Award -Winning Series: The Bluesuit Chronicles:

The War Comes Home
The New Darkness
Valley of Long Shadows
Day Shift
Unfinished Business
The Mystery of the Unseen Hand

Published & Award -Winning Essays and Short Stories:

"Losing Kristene"
"Riding the Superstitions"
"The Case of the Old Colt"
"Charlie's Story"
"The Mystery of Three"
"The Prospector"

Non-Fiction Book:
Song of the Waterwheel

Valley Of Long Shadows

Book 3 of The Bluesuit Chronicles

John Hansen

Valley Of Long Shadows
by John Hansen

This book is a work of fiction. Names, characters, locations and
events are either a product of the author's imagination, fictitious or
used fictitiously. Any resemblance to any event, locale or person,
living or dead, is purely coincidental.

Valley Of Long Shadows

JOHN HANSEN

To Patricia, my loving bride, who gave me a fresh start in life.
Te Amo, Mi Corazon

"The world is in a constant conspiracy against the brave. It's the age-old struggle: the roar of the crowd on the one side, and the voice of your conscience on the other."

~ General Douglas MacArthur

PROLOGUE

April 1970
McNeil Island Federal Prison
Washington State

BRUCE WILLIAM SANDS, inmate number 24785, a terrier-like punk, a pale, stocky, shifty-eyed loser with shaggy brown hair had been jailed fifteen times in seven states, all for penny-ante misdemeanors. By age twenty-eight he met the standard of what old-time cops called "a small-time hood." In the Missouri clan of habitual criminals of his birth, his half-sisters and half-brothers of the same mother but different fathers called him "the family jail bird."

Besides being born wrong, Sands grew up being cursed and knocked around by the long line of men who paraded through his mother's life. His childhood was bad enough for a book, but it was in juvenile reform school that his hatred for authority figures took root.

The beatings, cuffings, name-calling he received and privileges withheld for the slightest reasons by society's blue-coated guards exacted a heavy toll.

WEARY OF RISKING his life and freedom for small rewards, and crime being the only life-path he knew, Sands decided it was time for a change – he would move up to robbery. His luck forgot to change with him. His first holdup, a bank in Spokane, landed him on McNeil Island, the Northwest equivalent of Alcatraz, where bodies of icy salt water surrounded both island prisons, making escape impossible.

Sands hated having to work in the large vegetable gardens that fed the inmate population, overseen by armed, club-wielding guards, accompanied by German Shepherds trained to track down any convict who escaped into the island's woods.

When an opportunity for a shot at early parole release, and escape some of the forced labor came up, Sands and cellmates named John and Ed volunteered to participate in an experimental behavior modification program instituted in federal prisons in five states.

During intense group sessions, they were spoon-fed Marxist ideology and required to read and discuss the writings of Marx, Engels, Lenin and Mao.

The three played along with the program at first, but before long the three came to accept, and be transformed by communist doctrines. They seethed hatred for

America and the bourgeoisie, the upper and middle capitalist classes who owned most of the wealth and controlled the means of production. They vowed to resume their predations as soon as they were out but this time their actions would be acts of war, not crimes. They saw themselves returning to society as freedom fighters who would right the wrongs being inflicted by The Establishment on The People.

A sympathetic news media would herald them for their daring deeds. An adoring public would want to join them in liberating the exploited working classes from their upper-class oppressors.

Upon parole release, Sands worked as a journeyman machinist at Boeing through a generous program the company offered to rehabilitate prisoners from the cycle of crime and incarceration. He bought a battered gray late '50s Swedish-made Volvo with his first paycheck, preferring it to American-made cars because he favored Sweden's socialist-leaning politics.

He joined the Revolutionary Communist Party in Seattle, and betrayed the goodwill of his employers by spreading communist doctrine and unrest among his fellow workers.

At Boeing Sands was at best a marginal employee. His anger, criminal leanings and communist ideology simmered like bad stew on a stove. His abuse of company time by talking communist ideology to his fellow machinists rather than working, undermining the authority of his supervisors inevitably led to his being fired only six months after his parole.

By then he had Beatrice as his live-in paramour, a self-employed shop-keeper old enough to be his mother he met in a skid row bar on the Seattle waterfront. Now in her late forties, her long dark hair streaked with silver, face and figure rounded, her sensuality and reputation and local fame as a former stripper and more, drew the hip set to her, men especially. Never a believer in marriage, nor monogamy, Bernice purposely birthed and raised four children, each from a different bad man she selected to father a child for her.

Beatrice much preferred young men, especially if they were dangerous. To retain the attentions of a younger man, Beatrice kept Sands on a tight leash by lying to his parole officer that he was her full-time employee at her second-hand furniture and clothing store in Seattle's funky Fremont District.

IN RETURN FOR saving him from returning to prison, Sands agreed to be Beatrice's "kept" man. He ran business errands for her and satisfied her thirst for intimacy on demand. Truth be told, Sands was never Beatrice's employee; he was her hostage.

The arrangement suited Sands just fine. As long as he fulfilled his duties, intimate and otherwise, she met his needs for food, shelter, modest income, and the freedom to conspire with his former fellow inmates to prepare for insurrection.

Beatrice's lifestyle stuck in the craw of her four adult children, who had gone straight, bult careers and happy marriages with kids. Having observed this, Sands made himself scarce when her kids and grandkids came around, which, he observed, reignited Beatrice's lust for adventure and naughtiness.

For income beyond the pittance Beatrice doled out, Sands returned to burglary, the criminal craft of his youth. Unlike his earlier years, he had the hardening experience of jail and prison time under his belt, where older inmates schooled him in the finer points of criminality.

Without her knowledge, Sands scouted for homes and shops he would burgle later when he was out in her company van, marked with her company name and logo. He returned to the places he picked, disguised, driving a borrowed vehicle to 'liberate' the hard-earned wealth of others.

BY THE SUMMER of 1970, Sands shifted the focus of his burglaries to guns and ammunition to build an arsenal for the coming war. He and his two former cellmates John and Ed studied bomb-making from military and underground terrorist manuals, they rehearsed gunfighting tactics in the deep forests of East King County, where they shot at tree trunks, imagining them to be policemen.

Using police training manuals, they self-trained for parking lot shootouts at varying distances and positions, using their cars as barricades. As they did in prison, they practiced breaking out of police search positions to overcome an arresting officer and slit his throat.

As the season of clandestine war preparations neared the point of readiness, the trio researched which Establishment symbols to attack first. Banks topped the list, not only for symbolic significance, but for the cash that could be seized to fund the war. Next were robberies of state-run liquor stores. After that, symbolic bombings of luxury car dealerships, the headquarters of high-profile corporations, and the public utilities that served well-to-do neighborhoods would be bombed.

They collaborated on a manifesto to send to the press after their first strike. Claims of responsibility through press releases would be issued after each attack to inspire the working classes to revolt.

ANOTHER EX-FELON and a woman wanted for bank robbery in Oregon joined the trio, increasing the group's need for finances and armaments. As the primary source of weapons and income from trafficking in stolen goods, Sands expanded his predations to higher income neighborhoods.

BEATRICE SENT SANDS one day to pick up a used sofa

from a home in the historic Queen Anne neighborhood. Ungated, upscale and prosperous, it was located to the immediate north of Seattle's downtown. A van from a second-hand furniture store would hardly be noticed by the hip, well-to-do young residents who were perpetually updating their elegant 19th Century homes.

Marxist contempt writhed within him when he arrived at the two-story work of beautiful architecture and fine craftsmanship. A silver late model Jaguar XJ6 sat in the driveway as if waiting for its owners. Though the lady of the house graciously received him, her expensive dress and jewelry deepened his anger.

He fumed but said nothing when she led him past expensive new furnishings to the living room. She pointed to a perfectly fine mahogany leather couch. "We're donating it to Beatrice," she told him, "it's too old and stodgy for us. Use the front door, it's the only one wide enough."

Feeling dismayed and offended that the woman had so much money that she could throw away a couch nicer than any he had seen or even sat on, Sands held his silence. As he inched the couch out the front door, he heard her tell her teenage son, "Remember, Stewart, you have a doctor appointment at two p.m. tomorrow. I'll pick you up from school at 1:30. Your dad can't come because he's still in New York."

On behalf of the people you exploit, I'll get even with you, was Sands's thought as he returned to the house to hand the lady a receipt. He glared at her smiling face when she gave him a crisp new twenty-dollar bill as a tip and thanked him. He threw the tip at her feet and left.

THE INEQUITY OF the wealth in the lady's house when so many working people were struggling to keep food on their tables robbed Sands of sleep that night. *Marx and Engels were right,* he concluded, *people like this are the problem, they got what they have by exploiting others. They're enemies of the people and must be dealt with.*

He returned the next afternoon disguised in worn, tan bib overalls, striped railroad worker's cotton shirt, tattered brown canvas jacket, short-billed green wool cap, and round, metal rim granny glasses. No cars in the driveway. He rounded the block, parked against the curb, and entered the back yard on foot, carrying a cloth bag and a small prybar in the inside pocket of his jacket, surgical gloves in his pocket.

The wood frame basement window at the rear of the house slid up easily. As trim as he was, he could barely squeeze through it. As the drop to the concrete floor was over seven feet, he placed a wooden crate below the window as a step-up for a speedy exit.

Moving swiftly through the second-floor bedrooms, Sands seized antique gold jewelry, a solid gold man's pocket watch, gold chain attached, a wad of cash in a nightstand drawer, a pearl necklace, a diamond brooch and matching earrings from the master closet. From a jewelry box on the bathroom counter, he scooped gold rings, some set with rubies and emeralds. At the sound of a car outside he peeked through the curtain. It was the lady and her son, arriving in the silver Jaguar.

He raced down two flights of stairs to the basement, stood on the wood crate, placed the cloth bag outside the window and hoisted himself into the opening. His hip bone got stuck. Panic seized him—being caught meant completing his original sentence and more at McNeil Island.

On the floor above, he heard the front door open, then close, followed by footsteps. He twisted his hips to squeeze through the window opening. With all of his might and an adrenalin rush, Sands emerged, stomach-down, from the window onto the wet grass of the backyard. With no time to shut the window behind him, he dashed to his car in the alley behind the house and drove away, sweating and shaking.

HE CHANGED CLOTHES in a gas station restroom and stashed his disguise and his loot in the trunk of his Volvo. Sleep escaped him again that night, but this time it was because he feared a knock on the door by the men in blue.

When two days of running errands for Beatrice passed uneventfully, he felt it was safe to fence the stolen jewelry. His comrades needed the cash.

On the early afternoon of the third day after the

burglary, Beatrice told him, "Going to get my hair done. Be gone a couple hours at least. You're in charge until I get back."

Something is wrong, he thought. *Beatrice never gets her hair done. She can't afford it, so she wears it long, or in a bun, a turnoff for me because it makes her look older, or in a pony tail.*

His sense of alarm increased when she didn't kiss him before she left. *She always kisses me before she goes anywhere. For two days now her attitude toward me has been different. What's going on?* he wondered.

As soon as the shop was empty, Sands headed for the cash register. A frumpy-looking middle aged man, slightly overweight, gray mustache, glasses, wearing a tan trench coat and a short-brimmed plaid hat, entered the shop.

The man's presence sent a chill through Sands. *This guy's no customer. He ain't a cop either,* he told himself. "Can I help you find something, sir?"

The man in the trench coat had a predatory gleam in his eyes as he approached Sands. The man's right hand disappeared under his suit jacket and stopped. "My name is Tobias Olson, Bruce," he said, his right hand still under his suit jacket. "That's *Private Investigator* Tobias Olson to you, Bruce William Sands, Inmate number 24785."

Sands stared at him, dumbstruck, his flesh under his clothes trembling.

Olson kept staring as he withdrew his hand, holding a worn, brown leather wallet which he held in front of Sands. "Who do you suppose would be more interested in the future of the owner of this wallet, found in the basement of a home in Queen Anne, where you were on business three day ago? The Seattle Police, or you?"

CHAPTER ONE
Death On The Frontage Road

December 1970 - 2:00 A.M.
Bellevue, Washington

ON THE NORTH frontage road of US Highway 10, a wrecked, bullet-riddled green Ford Maverick, its grille wrapped around a telephone pole, contained two and a half dead bodies. A plume of steam from the radiator hissed as it rose into the frigid night air. The back window had been blown out from the inside by shotgun blasts. Glass fragments littered the trunk lid.

Blood drenched the seat behind and under the dead woman in the driver seat. More blood pooled under the dead man on the back floor behind the driver seat, cradling a double-barrel shotgun, his face shot to pieces.

Sergeant Jack Breen assigned two patrol officers to cordon off the westbound lane with barrier tape, set flares out and direct traffic. Two men from an out-of-town mortuary eased a bleeding, unconscious young woman from the front passenger seat onto a gurney.

A few feet behind the Maverick, two separate piles of six empty .38 Special cases twinkled red from rotating overhead police emergency lights.

Beyond the shell casings, Officers Hitchcock and Sherman stood, calm and unaffected by the cold because of adrenalin. They leaned against the front of Sherman's black-and-white cruiser, arms folded, watching the survivor being made ready for transport to the ER as they waited for the detectives to arrive.

"Think she'll make it?" Sherman asked.

Hitchcock shrugged and shook his head, staring at the gravel he pushed around with his shoe. "She's been gut-shot twice, Tom."

"But she'll be okay because you patched her up?"

"I did my best."

"Well, I vote for her pulling through," Sherman said in an effort to remain upbeat. He nodded at the shot-up Maverick. "Does this remind you of anything?"

"'Nam," Hitchcock replied. "You?"

"Saigon, sixty-eight."

"Tet, I assume?"

"Yep."

"Worried about what will happen to us?"

"What? Me, worry?" Sherman snickered.

"You know the third-floor faction will give us the rack and thumbscrews for this, Tom."

Sherman nodded and grinned as if he had just pitched a no-hitter in the major league playoffs. "Let's not forget the City Council. Most of them don't like us either!"

"They opened fire on us first," Hitchcock countered, "they got what they had coming – end of story. I heard the survivor tell Breen the missing girl from Everett is in the house the suspects came from."

"Ah, so *that's* why Otis showed up, spoke with Breen, and left in a hurry."

"Uh-huh, he'll find it, too."

Sherman's grin faded. "I'm worried about him going into a house of armed people alone."

"Joel doesn't need backup," Hitchcock said in his usual matter-of-fact manner.

CHAPTER TWO
Little Brown House

A HALF MILE from the scene of the ambush, Joel Otis idled his black-and-white cruiser along the streets of the sleeping working-class neighborhood of lower Eastgate, searching for a certain house.

The brisk cold air pouring through his open window sharpened his senses and allowed for better visibility and hearing, the heater on medium kept his legs warm. He spotted a house matching the survivor's description, a small brown rambler, single-car garage attached, on the street behind the gas station and the Denny's restaurant.

He hailed a paper boy cycling along on his route.

"Do you know who lives in this house, sonny?"

"Yes, sir," the kid replied, "a black man with a big white car lives there with a white woman and a lot of other people."

Otis radioed the address to Sergeant Breen. Using guarded words and Channel 2 because of listening reporters, he added "Lights are on inside, drapes drawn. I'm making contact."

"Be careful. No backup is available," Breen advised.

"Ten-four," he replied. He unzipped the side vent of his coat for quicker access to his Department-issue blued, four-inch bull-barreled Smith &Wesson Model 10 Military & Police .38 Special.

The doorbell didn't work. He knocked.

No response.

Flakes of peeling brown paint fluttered down when he pounded his fist on the thin wooden door. "Police officer! Open up!"

The door knob was locked.

The garage door lifted easily. The white early '60s Lincoln Continental inside left little room for walking around. Under the beam of his eight-cell Kel-Lite, he spotted cans of Conoco antifreeze, Valvoline motor oil and Mercon automatic transmission fluid, and a long black plastic funnel gathered dust on an eye-level shelf. The fluids, tools, and wood workbench reminded him of the one-man auto repair shop he apprenticed at during the summer before his junior year. *Whoever lived here before was a Ford man,* he surmised from the outdated brand of transmission fluid.

The interior of the Lincoln was empty and surprisingly neat. The registration on the driver side visor identified the owner as Tyrone Guyon. *Make that the late Tyrone Guyon, who made the mistake of ambushing*

Hitchcock and Sherman, now among the not-so-dearly-departed, never to be cold again, Otis noted.

He radioed Sergeant Breen: "Vehicle in the garage is registered to the suspect. Door from the garage to the house is unlocked. Request permission to enter the residence under exigent circumstances."

Permission granted. Be careful. No units available for backup.

"Thank you, Grandma," Otis muttered. He drew his gun, took one step into the kitchen, then stopped to assess the smells. Kitchen garbage, cigarette and marijuana smoke, dirty clothes – and something else.

The unplugged chrome coffee percolator and the open red can of MJB coffee on the counter added to the odors, as did the large glass ashtray overflowing with cigarette butts and ashes on the scarred wood kitchen table. Dirty dishes were piled in the sink up to the faucet. Even the yellow push-button phone on the counter had grime on it.

A creaking noise came from the other end of the house.

"Police officer! Is anyone here?"

No response.

He crept to the edge of the hallway, gripping his revolver in both hands in the low-ready position, waist-level, barrel pointed down, he stopped in the living room at the edge of the hall. His eyes noted the soiled tan corduroy couch, a Motorola TV, and a fake wood coffee table, stained from cigarette burns.

His back against the wall, Otis called out again.

"Police officer! If anyone's here, come out now!"

No response.

He heard the creaking again. *It's the house settling,* he concluded. He moved sideways down the hall.

The odors of sweat and marijuana met him when he flung open the first bedroom door. He swept the room and under the bed with his flashlight: Nothing.

He flipped the light switch. Unmade bed. His and her clothing and shoes on the floor. On the nearest nightstand to the door, a half-empty box of .38 Special hollow-point ammunition and a box of 12-gauge shotgun shells. On the other nightstand, a baggie of marijuana, a pipe, a half-empty box of .380 ACP full-metal-jacket pistol ammunition.

The second bedroom held only a mattress on the floor, covered by filthy sheets and a light blue blanket, a battered wooden dresser, an empty closet.

The bathroom told the ugly truth: A used hypodermic needle, a short length of surgical rubber tubing, a spoon burnt on the bottom with black residue and bloody cotton swabs laid on the counter.

A HEAVY BRASS padlock secured the door of the third bedroom. An odor Otis knew too well hit him when he kicked the door open with one strike of his size 13 boot. On a single bed flush against the opposite wall, a naked woman laid on her stomach, her face turned toward the wall. A sheet covered the lower half of her. She was beyond movement—way beyond.

There was no furniture in the room other than the bed. He recognized her the second he flipped the light switch. *Claudia somebody, the missing Seattle University student from Everett,* he nodded.

Purplish splotches of early-stage postmortem lividity dotted her back. Blood had pooled in the lowest parts of her body. He lifted her right wrist—stiffening from rigor mortis had begun. The hall thermostat read sixty-five degrees. *She died here about three, four hours ago,* the former combat medic concluded.

Without touching the body further, he leaned down to look at her more closely. Even in death he could tell that in life she had been a stunning beauty. About twenty-two, slender and shapely, delicate aquiline features and long, thick, light auburn hair. Even in death she exuded class. She gave him the impression of having come from a loving family.

Dark rage filled Otis as he assessed Claudia's remains. Emaciated from weeks of captivity, the bruises on her left cheek, left upper arm and both wrists told of abduction and torture.

The absence of clothing indicated the extent of the degradation and cruelty she suffered before her death. Four lengths of white nylon quarter-inch rope laid on the floor by the bed. Careful not to touch the body again, he visually examined the needle marks on her right arm. Claudia had been subjected to repeated sexual abuse and forced heroin injections until addiction reduced her to slavery.

He remembered seeing the victim's parents on the local evening news, tearfully begging anyone who had information regarding their daughter to come forward. To no avail the father posted a large cash reward for anyone with information leading to Claudia. Returning to his cruiser, he reported in guarded terms his findings to Sergeant Breen. He used up two rolls of film to photograph the scene.

Because this part of Eastgate was outside the city limits, he began cordoning the scene off with yellow plastic barrier tape. It would be a long wait. King County Sheriff's deputies, let alone the detectives, were few and far between in a sprawling jurisdiction.

As he continued working, he realized Hitchcock and Sherman made Department history tonight, for this was Bellevue's first officer-involved shooting. Two people died and the life of a third person hung in the balance.

Given the attitudes of some in the police brass and the city administration toward officers using force of any kind, he wondered what would happen to Sherman and Hitchcock, the younger brother he never had.

CHAPTER THREE
Scene of the Ambush

FOR TWO REASONS, Sergeant Jack Breen felt like pinching himself to be sure he wasn't dreaming. First, in less than an hour, he witnessed two of his officers prevail in a close-quarters gunfight in which they killed the people who ambushed them, then one of the officers saved the life of a gut-shot bystander, on whose information he sent Otis on a mission that resulted in finding the body of a missing woman in the dead suspects' residence.

Second, Breen's performance in a situation beyond his experience surprised him. He had preserved the scene, isolated the officers involved for the detectives, assigned two patrol officers to divert traffic to one lane until the Maverick could be towed away, ensured the lone survivor made it alive to the ER, and sent another officer with the victim to obtain evidence.

As he awaited the arrival of the city photographer,

the detectives and the coroner's "meat wagon," Breen returned to the Maverick for another look at what he knew wasn't a dream, but a landmark in city history that was sure to change the Department.

The dead woman in the driver seat was slumped forward on the steering wheel. She appeared to be in her twenties. Her seductive, vulgar sauciness reminded him of movie actress Mae West. Her left hand laid in her lap, right hand at her side, palm up. Her head rested on the steering wheel, turned toward the passenger side, mouth open, as if Death took her by surprise.

He peered again through the blown-out rear window of the Maverick at the dead man lying face-up on the floor behind the driver's seat. Despite the multiple gunshot wounds to his face, Breen recognized him from Seattle Police mugshots as Tyrone Guyon. The blood on his face was coagulating fast in the cold. His hands rested on a sawed-off double-barrel shotgun on his lap.

FRANK KILMER ARRIVED. A Bellevue cop for a couple years before he became the city photographer, Kilmer was no stranger to crime and death scenes. He began his trademark twisting his long, gray, waxed handlebar mustache as he inspected the scene to plan his documentation. Nodding and muttering "Um-hm, Um-hm," several times, punctuated with "I'll be damned," a couple times, he moved around the Maverick, dismayed at first, bobbing his head. He grinned smugly as he looked back at Sergeant Breen. "Looks like a scene from an action movie, Jack. Any of our guys hurt?"

Breen had turned the collar of his coat up, shoved his cold hands into the pockets and stamped his feet. "Nope," he replied with a brief shake of his head.

"Hitchcock and Sherman, I assume?" Kilmer asked, nodding at the two standing together.

"Yep."

"Ah, ha-ha-ha," Kilmer chuckled after a pause. "*Now* I get it. The two in the car made the mistake of ambushing the two *worst* officers they could have—both combat veterans."

"They won't make *that* mistake again," Breen joked, straight-faced, stamping his feet to keep them warm.

Kilmer grinned as he rubbed his hands together, "*This'll* pull some heads out of the sand at City Hall! Let me correct that—this is gonna *jerk* some heads out of the sand. Change is coming, Jack."

Breen scoffed and shook his head. "Don't bet on it, Frank."

The Korean War era Navy cameraman tape-recorded each step of his work. First, Polaroid shots of the car, the exterior, its location, the bodies inside, the bullet holes, the bloody interior. He repeated the routine with his trusty battered Pentax Spotmatic, loaded with Kodachrome color film, a Metz 85AF flashgun bracket-mounted to the camera. He switched to an 85 millimeter lens for close-up shots of bullet holes in the dashboard using black-and-white film for contrast, with a ruler next to the objects to show scale.

THE CORONER'S INVESTIGATOR arrived as Kilmer was finishing. Ian Barstow, a tall, lanky sort with thinning sandy hair, known to the cops for his distinct Canadian accent and a gallows sense of humor that resulted from years of collecting dead bodies, inspected the remains of Guyon and Driscoll.

"Bellevue's keeping us busy tonight, ay? Mack from our office is at a house about a mile from here where another of your officers found the body of the missing girl from Everett, ay – good *wurk* fellas!"

Barstow cheerfully rubbed his hands together as he saw the two dead in the Maverick. "Pardon the pun, but it looks like your boys got these two dead to rights!"

Breen cracked a grin, stamping his feet, hands in his coat pockets. "We offered 'em first aid, told 'em we had the kits in our cars, but they declined," he said, in keeping with his own brand of dry gallows humor his men knew him for.

"Hah! Imagine that, now" Barstow countered, glee in his voice. "Well, boys, I'd best be *aboot* my *wurk*!"

After taking photographs of the car and the bodies, Barstow bagged the hands of the dead woman in brown paper sacks, and sealed them at the wrists with tape. The driver's license in her purse identified her as Mae

Driscoll.

A DRIZZLE COLD enough to become snow began as the first detective to arrive helped Barstow remove Driscoll's body from the driver's seat to a gurney, getting blood on themselves as they slid it into the back of the coroner's station wagon.

Wearing surgical gloves, the detective removed the shotgun from Guyon's lap, opened the action for Kilmer to photograph the fired shells in the chambers, then sealed it in a large plastic bag for lab examination.

Barstow climbed into the back seat and sealed Guyon's hands in brown paper sacks. "This here fella wedged himself between the front and back seats. He's in there pretty tight, ay," he told the detective. "Rigor's setting in *fast* in this cold! Help me get him on a gurney before he stiffens up."

They both shivered in the bitter cold as they lifted Guyon's body off the back floor and squeezed it through the driver door a few inches at a time, exposing the puddle of blood under the body.

"Don't go yet, Detective," Barstow said between breaths after they laid Guyon on a gurney. "There's a revolver in his waistband and I think I feel a wad of cash in his pants pocket. I need you to witness my counting and sealing the money in an envelope."

They counted $2,800.00 in twenties, fifties and hundreds. The detective initialed and dated the sealed envelope.

Barstow smiled when he read the driver's license in Guyon's wallet. "Ah. I know a couple Seattle bulls who'll drink a toast to you boys for ending this guy's career. They've been after him for a lo-o-ong time."

AS BARSTOW LEFT for Seattle with two dead bodies, the detective spotted a small blue Colt automatic pistol lying on the right rear floor where Guyon's legs had been.

"Hey Frank, we missed this."

Kilmer photographed the pistol. The detective removed the magazine, careful to touch only the serrated surface of the slide to avoid smearing fingerprints when he ejected a live round from the chamber. He locked the slide back and placed each in a separate evidence envelope.

"Don't put your camera away yet, Frank." The detective pointed to a spent shell casing on the rear floor, where Guyon's body had been.

"Aha. Betcha the driver's little gun fired that little shell tonight," Kilmer speculated as his camera snapped more photographs.

"Yeah, but where did the bullet go is the question," the detective said as he used tweezers from his evidence kit to place the spent shell case into a coin envelope.

"Out the blown-out back window, most likely," Kilmer speculated.

HITCHCOCK AND SHERMAN were finally feeling the cold by the time Detective Sergeant Jurgens approached them, two large evidence envelopes in hand. "Tom, Roger," he nodded, "thank God neither of you is hurt. I have to take your guns for ballistic tests. Then head to the station to write your statements. You'll be issued temporary replacement weapons when you return to duty."

Hitchcock opened the cylinder of his service revolver, dumped the live ammo in and placed his weapon into the envelope. He was too nervous to say anything as he watched the detective supervisor write his name and badge number on the envelope, then seal it. Even Sherman's face reflected nervous anxiety as he surrendered his gun.

"Tom, go to the station and wait for me in one of the interview rooms," Sergeant Jurgens said. "Roger, you ride with me."

CHAPTER FOUR
The Lone Survivor

Overlake Hospital ER
2:30 A.M.

RHONDA KRINGEN, MD ignored the cold as she opened the back of the hearse as it backed into a parking slot. "Who is she?" Dr. Kringen asked no one in particular as she checked for vital signs.

"ID in her purse says she's Linda Ogilvie," Officer LaPerle answered.

"She's barely got a pulse! Get her inside. Quick!" The attendants and LaPerle rushed the gurney into the surgery room.

"Oxygen! IV! The clothes go!" Dr. Kringen shouted.

A nurse placed an oxygen mask over her nose and mouth as an intern rolled her side-to-side on the steel table to remove her coat before she could cut away the blood-soaked clothing with scissors.

With the introduction of oxygen, Linda's bluish

pallor receded. Dr. Kringen removed the bloody bandages from Linda's abdomen, revealing two bullet entrance wounds, one to the lower left rib cage, the other center-left, the location of the liver.

"Who patched her up?" Kringen asked the hearse attendants and LaPerle. "Whoever it was, did a good job. Stopped the bleeding. She just might make it."

"The officer was an Army medic," LaPerle replied.

"Oh. Well, it shows."

A nurse struggled to find a vein in Linda's arm big enough to receive an IV. Dr. Kringen drew blood and handed the vial to the nurse. "Take this to the lab for typing. Quick! We could lose her!"

Dr. Kringen and a nurse rolled the gurney into the X-ray room, "She's lost a lot of blood for someone so small. Get the on-call thoracic surgeon on the phone for me now!"

The X-rays revealed both bullets mushroomed, one lodged at the tip of the lower aorta, the other as it pierced her liver and spleen.

"Her blood type is O Positive," the nurse reported.

"That we have—more oxygen! Her breathing is slowing and she's turning blue again!"

The patient's breathing and pallor were restored with increased oxygen flow. Dr. Kringen glanced at LaPerle as she removed the first bullet. "What happened to this girl, officer?"

LaPerle shrugged. "She was in the wrong place,

with the wrong people at the wrong time."

"I asked *what* happened," she snapped.

"She was in the front seat with the driver, and a very bad man hiding in the back. Two of our officers recognized the car as a stolen and gave pursuit. They crashed into a telephone pole in their attempt to flee."

Dr. Kringen turned her attention to LaPerle, anxiety on her face. "And then?"

"The driver and the man hiding in the back opened fire on the officers when they approached to check for injuries. The officers returned fire at close range."

"How was this one involved?"

"She was front seat passenger—a bystander. She told us the driver shot her just before the crash. She passed out before she could say why. I'm here to receive her clothing and any bullets you remove as evidence."

Dr. Kringen froze, her bloody gloved hands on the victim's chest. She stared at LaPerle, fearing the answer to her next question: "Where did this happen?"

"Eastgate."

"And the officers involved are…?"

"Hitchcock and Sherman."

Her knees buckled. She gripped the edge of the steel table to steady herself. She stared at the floor. "Is Roger…I mean…are they…?"

LaPerle smiled, showing his teeth, yellowed from years of smoking Pall Malls and packing his gums with snoose. "Not to worry, Doc. Neither has a scratch.

Hitchcock was the one who stopped her from bleeding to death at the scene."

"Yes, I noticed. It's good work," Dr. Kringen said after a sigh of relief. "What happened to the two who started it?"

The poetic side of LaPerle that few people ever saw came out. He lifted his chin and gave the faintest smile as he replied, "Let it be said that they ran out of tomorrows."

CHAPTER FIVE
The Aftermath

HITCHCOCK WROTE HIS report in a separate room from Sherman. He could only remember the first shotgun blast and seeing most of the rear window disappear. He remembered firing his weapon once, yet there were six empty shell cases where he had been behind the Ford Maverick.

It came to him that a light spattering of glass on his chest followed the first blast. Seeing a man on the back floor, pointing a shotgun at him, came to mind as he began writing. Then more came back—*I kept shooting to stop Guyon from firing the shotgun again. Sherman and I both fired to stop him.*

When he finished, Detective Sergeant Jurgens took his report and asked him to write a second.

"More detail will come to mind as you keep writing, Roger."

Hitchcock sighed and shook his head. "Sorry, Sarge,

I'm out of steam. I'll be back after a few hours in the rack." He headed for the door.

"We'll set an appointment for you with a psychologist."

He stopped and looked back at Jurgens. "A shrink? What for?"

"For you and Sherman, of course. You guys just killed two people in a gunfight at point-blank range, and you aren't bothered?"

"Tell the City to save its money," he scoffed. "I need sleep."

THE SIGHT OF Jamie, his German Shepherd-Husky mix waiting for him in the driveway, rain-soaked, tail wagging, gave him a second wind. He toweled and fed him, changed into his gray sweatshirt and pants, and thick cotton socks.

With a glass of Old No. 7 with ice and his feet up on his battered wooden coffee table, he rubbed Jaime's furry head as he drank. Only one thing bothered him – he felt naked, stripped, and pre-judged to come home with an empty holster.

In the solitude of his abode, he relived the moments before he started shooting: The rear window exploding outward, glass fragments pelting him, Tyrone Guyon on the back floor, aiming a shotgun at him, the second shot about to go off. *Where were they going at that hour?* he wondered.

Gayle, his informant, came to mind. This had been her first case. Only a few hours ago, she warned him that Guyon showed his gun to a motel maid and told her he intended to kill a white police officer—any white officer with it. Because of Gayle's bravery, Guyon and his female partner were dead and the intended deaths of one or more police officers had been prevented.

Drowsiness came over him as cold, gray daylight seeped through the windows. He mustered the energy to make a call.

"Hello?" Gayle's voice sounded thick with sleep.

"It's me, Roger."

"Oh, hi."

"Guyon and Mae Driscoll tried to kill me and my partner last night," he said bluntly. "They're both dead. I want to thank you and tell you about it before you hear it on the news. You saved lives last night, and I am grateful."

He noticed his words came slowly with slurred, thick pronunciations. *Exhaustion's caught up with me*, he realized as he heard Gayle gasp. "Are you all right? You don't sound normal," she asked.

"I'm fine. I just need some shut-eye," he said, becoming groggier by the minute. "I'll call you back in a few hours." He paused. Even his thought processes were slowing. "Don't worry. No one knows you're my Mata Hari."

"Tell me what happened!"

"Later, Gayle...I'm fading."

The phone rang again right away. "Hey, Roger, its Eve. I heard the news. Are you all right? You aren't hurt, are you?"

"Fine. Just trying to cut a few Z's," he said, his head starting to nod.

"What! You can sleep after a shooting?"

"I'm wiped out," he said, exhaling. "By the way, thanks for the warning you gave me about Lieutenant you-know-who."

"Oh, yeah. I hear the nasty little twerp is *very* busy this morning. We'll talk later," she promised.

He fell into a dreamless slumber as soon as he unplugged his phone.

A PERSISTENT POUNDING on his sliding glass door forced him out of a dreamless sleep an hour later. He recognized the frantic voice outside as Rhonda's.

"Roger! Wake up! Let me in!"

Stiff, numb and relaxed by his morning meeting with Mr. Jack Daniels, he crawled out of bed and shuffled to the door like an old man. Rhonda threw her arms around him when she stepped inside. He tried to put his arms around her trim waist and hug her but even his arms were tired.

He managed a faint smile. "Still in your hospital scrubs, but where's your stethoscope, Doctor?"

"What? How can you make jokes after what

38

happened?"

"As Mark Twain once said, 'The rumors of my demise are greatly exaggerated,'" he quipped, giving her a playful smirk.

"Stop it! I tried calling you, but no answer. You're not hurt, are you? What exactly happened? How are you doing?"

"I unplugged my phone. I'm not hurt, and I'm trying to sleep."

Rhonda stood back a step, shocked even more. "What's this? I ask what happened and how you are, and all you say is you unplugged your phone, you're not hurt and you want to sleep? Tell me what happened!"

"We made a stop on a stolen car."

She stared at him, dismayed. "Stolen car?! Come *on*! I treated the survivor. She's been shot twice and is not expected to live. The news says it's more than a stolen car—a lot more. I can't believe neither of you are injured!" She ran her hands over his body, partly to check him for injuries.

He gave her a lustful smirk. "Keep checking, Doc."

She reached under his sweatshirt as a new wave of exhaustion came over him. "Sorry, but I'm thirty hours without sleep. I—"

"Of course, forgive me. You're coming down from long hours and a major adrenalin rush. As your *personal* doctor I can attest that your boxer's body is intact. Sleep.

I'll check on you later. They better give you both some time off," she said.

He grinned drowsily as she gave her blue knight a forceful kiss on the lips, and left.

† † †

TOM SHERMAN CALLED his wife from the station to say he would be home late, leaving out the details. He came home two hours later, finding her still there.

"Hi, hon," he said, hiding his surprise by kissing her. "You're late gettin' to work today?"

Karen stood in front of him and shook her head, running her hands over his wiry frame, checking for injuries. "Told 'em I'm not coming in today," she said, her voice husky with emotion.

Sherman took her in his arms, but deep exhaustion displaced the familiar rush of surviving being shot at. Every cell, every nerve in his body screamed for rest, but his wife needed him. "How come?" he asked thickly, teasing her with the last of his energy.

She stepped back, shocked and more than a little irritated. "My *husband* got shot at again, that's why," she said defiantly. "This time he is *home*, not Vietnam. This time you're—" she broke into tears. "Hold me, Tom. Someone tried to kill you, and I'm angry, and scared."

Sherman slipped his arms around his trembling wife, thinking of a round of intimacy with her, but his body said *uh-uh*.

CHAPTER SIX
The Blue Judas

AT THE SCENE, the rain stopped. It was the pre-dawn version of daylight. A single degree colder would ice the roads. Sergeant Breen, exasperated from standing in the cold and dodging questions from pesky reporters until the Maverick, sealed with evidence tape, was towed away at last, followed by a detective.

He noticed Lieutenant Bostwick's open office door and the lights on when he entered the station. *A janitor must've left it like this,* he thought. He spotted a memo in plain view on the desk when he stepped in to turn off the lights. All memorandums are to be typed. This drew his attention because it was hand-written. Breen's face flushed red as he read several pages of correspondence between Bostwick and a junior member of the City administration.

Breen hurried to make copies before Bostwick arrived. He slid the copies into a manila envelope he marked FOR YOUR EYES ONLY in large letters and slipped it under Captain Delstra's locked office door, keeping the originals.

Moments later he saw Lieutenant Bostwick coming down the hallway, his beady eyes bulging, breathing through his open mouth like a fish.

"Oh, Jack, I think I got distracted and left my office door open yesterday. Some important papers are missing from my desk. Do you know anything about it?"

"Why yes, Rowlie," Breen said, smiling as he would a rat in his home he finally caught. "When I saw lights on in your office and your door standing open, I saw important papers on your desk."

"Yes, yes, thank you, Jack!" Bostwick gushed, looking partly relieved. "Uh, where are the papers now?"

"I didn't know when you'd be back, and there's lot going on this morning because of the shooting, so to protect you by keeping them safe," Breen said, shrugging. "I slid them under the door into Captain Delstra's office."

Bostwick's jaw went slack. His flaccid jowls quivered. "You-you gave them to...who?"

"Captain Delstra, of course. To keep them safe, so..."

The color drained from Bostwick's face. He collapsed onto the wooden public bench in the hallway, staring at the floor like a condemned man. As soon as Breen left, he went into his office and plopped into his chair, pondering his fate.

A practical joker by nature, Breen knocked on Bostwick's door five minutes later with a manila envelope in his hand. He ran his other hand over his blond crew-cut, faking embarrassment.

"Forgive me, Rowlie. I'm so tired, I forgot I put your papers in *this* envelope for safekeeping. Here they are. Sorry for any confusion I may have caused."

Bostwick looked like a drowning man who had been thrown a life ring at the last possible moment. "You mean you didn't give these papers to Captain Delstra?"

"*Those* are the papers I found, Lieutenant," Breen said, evading the whole truth.

"Thank you, thank you, Jack," Bostwick said, relief on his face.

"No problem. By the way, Rowlie, the two officers who prevailed in the city's first gunfight when two armed criminals ambushed them last night? You know – Hitchcock and Sherman? They're both unhurt and doing fine. Thanks for asking and showing your concern," Breen mocked.

Bostwick stared at Breen, caught off guard. "Huh? Oh-Oh yes! Yes of course! I really was concerned for them, of course I was, but... ah, well, *so* glad they're fine," he said, faking a thin smile. "Now if you'll excuse me..."

AS SOON AS Breen left, Bostwick's phone rang. He smiled when he answered. "Yes, of course," he chuckled. "Everyone in the station is filled with excitement and shock, but for us, what luck, eh?"

He paused to listen. "Oh, I agree, I agree. This is a *rare* opportunity. Not to be wasted!"

He paused again, then smiled. "Yes! Yes! This shouldn't be difficult to do," Bostwick said, bubbling with excitement. "What's that? Oh, a shooting review board doesn't exist here because the Department has never had a shooting like this before where someone died."

After another pause, Bostwick exclaimed," Yes! I'll start this morning and make sure I'm in charge. We'll rid the Department of *two* veterans! If we can get them prosecuted and sued by the victims' families, it will open the door to rid ourselves of others like them! I wouldn't miss this for anything," Bostwick said, glee in every word.

CHAPTER SEVEN
Anatomy of a Shooting

7:00 A.M.
The Autopsy Room
Harborview Hospital

FOURTEEN CADAVERS, RANGING in age from teens to the sixth decade, laid supine, each on a stainless steel table on wheels, in different stages of decomposition. The causes ran the gamut from gunshot, stabbing, overdose, car accident, one by drowning. Like slabs of hanging beef in a slaughterhouse, each cadaver had its weight and height written in large numbers on the side of the abdomen in black felt pen. The case number was written on an evidence tag attached to a big toe.

The lean, dapper man in his fifties with a full head of salt-and-pepper hair who entered the autopsy room was the county coroner, the renowned pathologist, Dr. Kenneth Banker. He gave a friendly nod to Sergeant Jurgens and Detective Small.

"This is Bellevue's first officer-involved shooting, I understand?"

"That it is, Doc," Jurgens replied.

"We'll start with the male decedent," Dr. Banker said, "and welcome to the club."

Dr. Banker posted Guyon's X-rays on a light board. "No abnormalities are evident in the torso," he said, "but we have two slugs in the cranium."

Dr. Banker's assistant, a slim, attractive brunette in her mid-thirties, whose name tag read: JANET MORRISON, used a scalpel to make one large Y-shaped incision from each shoulder across the chest, then down to the pubic bone. She spread open the skin and checked to see if any ribs were broken. Next, Morrison split the sternum using rib shears, opened the chest cavity and examined the lungs and heart for abnormalities. She took a second blood sample directly from the heart, then removed and weighed each organ in the chest cavity.

The putrid smell of partially digested food, urine and stool caused Jurgens and Small to retch when Morrison repeated the process for the spleen, stomach and intestines. She removed the brown paper bags from Guyon's hands and placed fingernail scrapings in small labeled envelopes. She swabbed his hands with alcohol patches to detect gunpowder residue and cut samples of head hair from different areas of his scalp for later comparison.

Morrison paused to study the gunshot wounds to Guyon's face. "If all three shots came from the same gun, the officer should get a medal for marksmanship," she said. "They're no more than an inch and a half apart– impressive."

"Ten bucks says all three came from Hitchcock," Small told Jurgens.

Jurgens shook his head. "No dice. I went shooting with Roger once."

Small noticed Morrison's wedding ring under the plastic glove on her left hand as she cut around Guyon's hairline with a scalpel and peeled the scalp over his face. *Wonder what she says when her hubby asks, 'so how was your day, dear?* he snickered to himself. She put goggles on, picked up a circular power saw, put goggles on. "You guys better step back."

She flipped the power switch. The blade emitted a high-pitch whine which deepened to a low growl as it bit into the skull. A spray of bone dust arose as the saw went around the skull cap, which Morrison removed, then lifted out the brain with both hands.

Dr. Banker dissected the brain to locate the two bullets the X-ray revealed. Using tweezers, he put them in a metal tray. "Typical thirty-eight slugs," he said. "We have three gunshot wounds, only two slugs. The third bullet should be somewhere inside the car. Each of these would be fatal. The body is otherwise unremarkable."

THE PROCEDURE WAS repeated on Mae Driscoll's corpse. Dr. Banker held up a bullet he removed from Driscoll's aorta. "Thirty-eight again. These are longer than most police bullets. Your department must use heavy slugs."

Sergeant Jurgens nodded. "That we do," he said.

"This one caused rapid terminal bleeding. Death would come in a minute or less."

Dr. Banker removed another bullet from Driscoll's spine. "This one struck the spine at C3, causing instant paralysis for everything below the neck, like turning off a power switch. Whatever she was doing when this hit, she couldn't finish," he explained.

"Makes sense," Jurgens said. "Sitting in the driver seat, this Mae West lookalike turned around to shoot the cop in the back window, then one of our bullets struck, her gun went off prematurely, the bullet went wild, the gun fell from her hand and landed on the back floor of the car."

"She does resemble Mae West, doesn't she?" Dr. Banker observed. "Your analysis seems likely. I believe the second bullet I removed probably hit her first."

INSIDE IBSEN TOWING across 116th Avenue from City Hall, two detectives in mechanics overalls and surgical gloves worked with the city photographer inside the

Ford Maverick. They inserted aluminum rods with strings at one end into bullet holes to determine the trajectory of each round.

Using needle nose pliers, they recovered four .38 slugs from the driver side of the dashboard and three more from the lower portion of the driver seat.

Captain Holland arrived. He looked at the shot-up vehicle with dried blood covering the front seat and rear floor, too amazed to say anything at first.

"Any progress?" he asked.

"We're almost finished, Captain. What we found was revealing," Larry Meyn, the senior detective replied. "For starters, we found another bullet, one of ours, that entered the lower driver seat from the rear. It had blood on it, indicating it passed through the suspect who was on the rear floor, who fired a shotgun at the officers."

Holland listened, at a loss for words.

"The detectives who searched the interior at the scene when it was dark recovered two .380 caliber cartridge cases on the middle of the front seat," Detective Meyn explained, "which accounts for the driver shooting the passenger. Another .380 cartridge case was recovered from the middle of the back seat, which verifies Sergeant Breen's observation that the driver turned in her seat to shoot Hitchcock."

"Good work, I'm impressed."

"Yes, Captain, but probably due to weather

conditions, dead and wounded bodies at the scene, our guys missed the bullet hole in the headliner above the rear window on the passenger side," Meyn said. "Here, in a lighted, controlled environment, we noticed the headliner fabric had a bullet hole in it. We removed much of the fabric and recovered the bullet, which lacked the velocity to pass through the roof of the car."

"Aha," Holland acknowledged, nodding his head, arms folded because of the cold. "Go on."

"Then," Meyn continued, "we used a string attached to a trajectory rod inserted from the dent in the roof to determine the bullet path. This confirmed the bullet came from the driver seat area. So the driver had to turn around in her seat to shoot at Hitchcock where he stood on the right side of the rear window."

"Which had been blown out by a shotgun blast from the inside," Captain Holland said, completing Meyn's explanation.

He stared in disbelief at the headliner fabric and the .380 slug in Meyn's hand for a few seconds. "Do you think the driver missed Hitchcock because she was in a panic?"

"We don't know yet," Meyn replied as he took off his overalls and put away his tools. "We've recovered spent slugs from the driver seat and the dash. It'll be up to the state crime lab to determine which bullets came from which gun in order to account for the actions of each officer."

"Are you done here?" Holland asked.

"Yes, sir. I'm heading back to the hospital now to see if I can interview the survivor before she dies," he replied.

CHAPTER EIGHT
A Dying Declaration

5:50 P.M.
Intensive Care Unit
Overlake Hospital

AFTER WAITING SEVERAL hours, Detective Meyn studied what was left of Linda Ogilvie, still-pretty, but a drug-emaciated young woman with mouse-brown hair and fine features. He had almost given up hope that she would awaken when suddenly she opened her eyes. Only the rhythmic hush of the respirator, the faint bleeping of the heart monitor and the soft foot-falls of regular nurse visits intruded upon the silence in Linda's room. She looked at Meyn with hollowed-out eyes that told of addiction and abuse and wanted to know who he was.

He pressed the call button.

"Linda, I'm Detective Larry Meyn, Bellevue Police

Department," he said softly, showing his badge. "I'm here to ask what happened that you were shot twice. Are you able to talk now?"

She nodded.

"Have the doctors informed you regarding your medical condition?"

She struggled for the strength to speak. "They tell me unless a new liver from a donor can be found, I will die," she croaked.

A nurse entered. "Linda is awake now and is willing to tell me what happened," Meyn told her. "Please summon Dr. Townsend."

Minutes later Meyn touched her forearm. "Linda, Dr. Townsend is with us as a witness regarding your condition and to this interview. With your permission I will record it. Do you agree?"

"Yes," she whispered.

He pressed the start button of his tape recorder. When the spools started turning, he stated the date, time and place, introduced himself, Linda and Dr. Townsend, then placed the microphone on the bed close to Linda.

"Linda Ogilvie, are you aware that you are being recorded?"

"Yes."

"Is this recording being made with your consent?"

"Yes."

"Please state your name, your age, where you are

now and why you are here."

After a short pause, Linda began in a weak voice. "My name is Linda Ogilvie, I'm twenty-one years old. I'm in the hospital because Mae Driscoll shot me."

"Linda, are you aware that your doctors say you are dying, that there is nothing more they can do for you?"

"Yes," she said with a solemn nod.

"I am now asking Dr. Townsend to verify his presence and Linda's statements regarding her medical condition." Meyn gestured to the doctor.

"My name is Doctor Roy Townsend. I'm a staff physician at Overlake Hospital. Linda Ogilvie is my patient. Linda is correct in stating that as a result of gunshot wounds, her medical condition is terminal if a liver donor cannot be found."

Meyn spoke into the recorder. "Thank you, Dr. Townsend. Now Linda, please tell us how this happened."

Tears filled Linda's eyes. She took a ragged breath and began sobbing. Meyn held her hand and patted her forearm. In a few moments she wiped her tears and began, "I became... addicted to heroin...through Tyrone Guyon and his girlfriend... Mae...Mae Driscoll...," she said, struggling to speak. "Last...last night we headed to...Seattle... to buy...more heroin... A cop car...tried to stop us. Tyrone yelled at Mae not to...stop...to lose them... But...the-the cops–Tyrone said he would kill a cop... I wanted-wanted...out of the car. Tyrone hid in the back...with big gun...said he'd kill the cop. I fought...with Mae to stop the car... tried taking the keys... she shot me... gun from her purse. I remember a crash... a lot of gunshots. Mae fired her gun toward the back. I was...too-too scared, too hurt to move." Linda stopped speaking.

"Linda, where is the heroin Guyon was going to buy?" Meyn asked.

"I was so scared when we left the house. I heard them..."

"You heard them do or say what?" Meyn pursued when she stopped speaking.

Linda broke down, sobbing. "They said they were going to sell me to Marcellus..."

"Who is Marcellus?"

"Tyrone, he was-was out... His source, Marcellus, Mar-Mar...Marcellus. Marcellus Whitney... His house... Old house... Central District."

Knowing there might not be another chance to talk to Linda, Meyn kept probing. "Can you describe the house?"

Linda's eyelids drooped. After a pause of several seconds, she gathered enough strength to reply: "Small. White...house...green-green door. Twenty... third street..." She lapsed into unconsciousness.

Dr. Townsend checked her vital signs as Meyn ended the recording.

"Well, Doc?" Meyn asked.

Dr. Townsend shook his head as he looked at Linda but said nothing.

Meyn waited expectantly, then asked again, "Well?"

"All I can say is that I hope you got everything you need, Detective."

Meyn gathered his notebook and equipment. He was headed for the door when Dr. Townsend said, "I don't envy you your work, Detective."

The doctor's words stopped Meyn for a second, his back toward Dr. Townsend, then left without looking back, for he had no words.

CHAPTER NINE
Shock Waves

NEWS-HUNGRY REPORTERS, television cameramen and newspaper photographers swarmed City Hall, the scene of the shootout, and the house where Otis had found Claudia Masconi's body. Hospital security personnel prevented them from disrupting Linda Ogilvie.

A big-city style shooting in a sleepy suburb was fresh meat for members of the press. Reporters hounded the Department for background information about Hitchcock and Sherman. They were frustrated that half of Hitchcock's military service record was classified and Sherman's record was barely more available.

The television coverage reached the point of nauseating absurdity when a reporter asked Sherman's fifth grade teacher "what kind of little boy was Tom Sherman? Any problems? What kind of grades did he get? Did you ever have to discipline him?"

Calls from reporters, news stations, and City Council members jammed the Department's phone lines. It became necessary to pull the Department's five detectives off their regular cases to investigate the shooting. Everyone, from Records clerks to top level Brass, wished another major news event would break to send the news-hounds trundling away.

† † †

IT WAS MID-AFTERNOON, gray, grim and chilly as usual when Hitchcock arose from a deep sleep. He let Jamie out and reheated yesterday's coffee. His phone rang as soon as he plugged it in. *Probably Steve Miller, my reporter buddy for the Bellevue paper*. He was in no mood to talk to a reporter, even Miller. He almost didn't answer, but he smiled when he did.

"Roger? It's Allie! After hours of calling, I finally reach you! I called the station but they wouldn't tell me anything. If I knew where you live, I would come over to check on you. Are you all right?"

The musical lilt and the concern for him in her voice made him smile. "I unplugged my phone because I needed sleep, and yes, I'm fine now, because you called."

Her ragged sigh of relief told him she'd been crying. "I'm so glad you're not hurt, but I want proof. Can I bring you anything?"

"I'm going to be tied up for a while with all that's

going on. How about you? Any changes?"

"No changes here. My eyes need to see you, see that you really *are* all right. Come by the Corral when you can, or at least call me. Please."

"I will."

"Promise?"

He smiled again, encouraged by the promise he heard in her voice. "Yes, Allie I promise."

His phone rang again. "Hey, Roger. Steve Miller, *Bellevue American*. I'm sure you were sitting by your phone, anxiously awaiting my call."

Hitchcock grinned. Miller had hired on at the weekly paper the same time he joined the Department. "Ah, Steve. They told me to never give my phone number to a reporter, but as usual I didn't listen. What's up?"

"How are you doing?"

"Fine. You?"

"Uh, I'm not the one who was in a gunfight mere hours ago. Two people died and you tell me you're *fine*?"

"Except for several *unnecessary* interruptions, I slept just fine after I came home," Hitchcock hinted.

Miller paused. "You were able to sleep because of your Vietnam experiences, I presume?"

No answer.

"Sorry, I forgot you veterans don't talk about the

war, even among each other. What can you tell me about the shooting?"

"Am I off the record and not being recorded?"

"Absolutely."

He filled Miller in on the details as he remembered them.

"Thanks. Now I'll share with you what I learned from my contact at the Coroner's Office. The autopsies were done this morning but the reports won't be out until tomorrow or the next day. I'm told Mae Driscoll died from two bullets which entered her back through the driver seat. Guyon was on the floor behind the driver seat, so either you or Sherman killed Driscoll when you were shooting at Guyon."

Hitchcock fell silent at the thought he might have killed a woman. Killing Guyon was his intention, he aimed his gun solely at Guyon, who fired at him. He had no problem living with that—he had killed men before. But harming women went against the code he had been raised under. The thought that one of his bullets went through Guyon, then the front seat and killed the woman in the driver seat would torment him now, even though the dead woman was armed and shooting.

"Anything else?" He asked Miller.

"Between the bodies of Guyon and Driscoll and the Ford Maverick they were in, twelve rounds of pistol fire from you and Sherman have been accounted for. Guyon caught three bullets to the head. Driscoll caught two.

Others were misses that lodged in the driver seat or the dashboard. Guyon fired both barrels of his shotgun. That, plus at least three shots were fired by the driver but only two hit the passenger. So much gunfire at close range must have been fierce," Miller said. "Any comments?"

"What about the passenger, Linda somebody?" Hitchcock asked, dodging the question.

"In Overlake's ICU, fighting for her life."

"And the girl in the house?"

"Dead. Cause undetermined at this time. My guess is heroin overdose. She's been identified as Claudia Masconi, the Seattle U co-ed from Everett who disappeared while bar-hopping with some friends in the Central District."

"Thanks, Steve. I'm glad you called."

"One more thing before you go..."

"Yes?"

"There's a reporter at one of the Seattle papers who says he's getting a lot of inside information from a member of your Department. None of it good."

He sat up straight. "Who is it?"

"He won't say, but he is saying that the source told him certain people in the city administration plan to use the shooting to fire you and Sherman, and have you prosecuted."

Hitchcock's heart pounded. He could hardly believe his ears. "How credible is this reporter, Steve?"

"Very experienced, but biased. He thinks all cops are bad. Watch your back, Roger."

"Noted."

He hung up the phone, dazed. *It has to be Bostwick. Who else? But Steve said 'people' in the City, as in plural, want him and Tom prosecuted.*

More details of the shooting came to mind as he hung up. He touched the framed black-and-white photograph on his nightstand of his father, then drove to the station where he found Detective Captain Holland at his desk.

"I remember more of what happened last night. I'm here to write another statement."

"Good man, Roger. Use any desk over there to write, take as much time as you need."

When he finished, Captain Holland told him, "Per the Chief, you and Sherman are on administrative leave with pay for two weeks. Your sergeant's been notified, so he won't expect you two tonight. If you go out of town, leave us the number where you can be reached. From what we can see at this point, this is a clean shooting, so if you're worried, don't be."

A SENSE OF impending doom came over Hitchcock as he returned to his El Camino, parked in the city library parking lot, facing the station. He put the key into the ignition but didn't turn it. Conspiracies by organized crime groups were a fact of life in protecting the public, sort of cops-and-robbers on a larger scale. But plots by hidden officials within the city and the Department to betray and persecute those who do their job was a level of treachery he couldn't grasp. Now that he thought about it, he wondered if he detected a changed attitude underneath Captain Holland's friendly demeanor.

Should I believe the captain that we have nothing to worry about? What Sherman and I did was by the book, it was even witnessed by our supervisor. Are the unnamed people Steve Miller warned me about, who want to persecute us, motivated politically, or do they have an interest in the drugs coming into the city? If so, it explains why we can't get approval to create a narcotics squad or an intelligence unit when the situation demands it. Who the hell can I trust besides Otis, Walker and Sherman?

None of it made sense. Fighting feelings of paranoia, Hitchcock drove to the Pancake Corral, wanting to see Allie. She wasn't there.

CHAPTER TEN
The Payoff

ISOLATED FROM POLICE headquarters in another downtown office building, Milo Lewis, the Seattle Police Narcotics Unit's newest sergeant, typed a search warrant affidavit for the residence of Marcellus Whitney. To lessen his cop appearance after his transfer from Patrol, Lewis grew his hair out and had it permed into an Afro hairstyle. He completed his transformation by retiring his razor to give himself the chic "underground" look of a several-days-old beard.

Atwood Morgan, the Narcotics Unit's lieutenant, a dapper, fortyish executive type, pinstripe suits, ties and oxford shoes, sat across from Lewis, his feet up on the desk, sipping coffee.

"Bellevue hand-delivered the case on Whitney on a silver platter this morning," Morgan said.

Lewis kept typing. "I know," he said. "Their captain of detectives is tight with the chief of our intel unit, so the order to act on it now came from the top. We sent Rocky, our sleaziest snitch, into Whitney's place where he made a controlled buy a couple hours ago. Said he saw a mother-lode of heroin and cocaine. While Rocky was inside, we saw a lot of people coming and leaving in minutes."

"Got the plate numbers of their cars?"

"You bet," Lewis replied.

Lieutenant Morgan nodded, loosened his tie and sipped his coffee again. "Thanks to Bellevue," he said, "Guyon and Mae what's-her-name are pushing up daisies. Hopefully we'll put Whitney in the tank by day's end."

Lewis chuckled as he typed. "The facts are so tight it squeaks. Like a movie."

"Yeah?"

"True fact."

"Tell me."

Sergeant Lewis told Morgan the facts of the shooting as he knew them. "Both the Bellevue officers were in Vietnam," Lewis added as he ended the story. "They emptied their guns, smokin' 'em both, just as their sarge arrives and sees the whole thing go down. Only the hooker is alive when the shooting stops. Apparently Guyon's madam shot her, but she survives because one of the Bellevue guys was a combat medic in the Army. She lived to give a dying statement at the hospital which they recorded and gave us the transcript all in the same day."

Lieutenant Morgan leaned back in his chair, hands behind his head, as he listened to Lewis. "If I ever go into script writing after I retire, *that's* a scene I'd use."

Lewis removed his search warrant affidavit from his typewriter. "The next chapter is ours to write, Lieutenant," he said, ripping the affidavit out of his typewriter, "and I'm starting right now."

CHAPTER ELEVEN
Truth or Consequences

KING COUNTY SUPERIOR Court Judge William "Wild Bill" Conklin, known for his blunt style and crusty comments to defendants, their attorneys, therefore a favorite of the cops, signed the search warrant for Marcellus Whitney's residence.

Lewis and his team of detectives and two uniformed officers surrounded the white dilapidated clapboard house in the Central Area.

He shouted, "Lewis–Police! Search warrant!" as he and a uniformed officer crashed through the front door, guns drawn. Marcellus Whitney and two white men were sitting on a couch in the living room. Lines of off-white powder on a mirror and rolled bills as straws were on the coffee table.

"Hands in the air. Fingers spread!" Lewis said. "You're all under arrest for Investigation of Violation of Uniform Controlled Substances Act."

The three raised their hands as detectives and uniformed officers streamed into the house. They handcuffed and searched each of them.

"Well, well, what have we got *here*?" Lewis said, grinning with relish as he removed a loaded .357 Magnum revolver from the front of Whitney's waistband.

"I've gotcha for being a felon in possession of a firearm, so there goes your next five years, Whitney. Let's see what your customers are packing."

Lewis handed the revolver to a uniformed patrol officer and patted down the first white male suspect, finding a similar revolver in a holster under the man's shirt.

The suspect trembled as Lewis held the revolver up to his face. "If even one felony is on your resume, your ole lady better start looking for someone else to keep her warm on winter nights. Hopefully she'll find someone younger and better looking than you."

"Same goes for you," Lewis said as he removed a 9mm Colt automatic from the waistband of the second white male suspect.

"Take these two in for booking," he ordered the patrol officers. He detained Whitney while the patrol officers took the others outside.

A further search of the immediate area by Lewis and his other two narc agents of the area within Whitney's reach yielded over one pound of cocaine, along with a

.45 automatic under the couch cushions where Whitney had been sitting.

Lewis found a fully automatic Ingram 9mm submachine gun and two loaded magazines in a duffel bag along with Whitney's wallet in an upstairs bedroom. He went downstairs and held it up to Whitney's face.

"Some gun, *old man*. Full automatic, too. That puts you in *Federal* territory. Bad, bad, bad," he said, shaking his head. "And the *serial number* has been drilled through! Now you're *buried* in Federal territory! Gotta hand it to ya, Marcus, when you dig yourself into a hole, you dig deep! You got yourself a second charge here, one that means *federal time*, old man. I'm calling you '*old man*' now, wanna know why?"

Whitney turned his head away.

"Don't turn away. I'm helping you out, here, Whitney," Lewis cooed with heavy sarcasm.

Whitney scoffed. "The hell, I'm in handcuffs."

"Yeah, but you're moving up. Belly-chains and leg shackles are next. But *please* don't say anything."

"Say what?"

"I'm calling you '*old man*' because that's what you'll be by the time you get out, if you ever do. That is, upright and breathing, not in a coffin. Your hair, if any is left, will be gray and you'll shuffle along on a cane from all the knife wounds you'll get for being a snitch."

Whitney scoffed again as he tilted his head back.

"You think I'm so scared I'll beg to cut a deal with you, huh? Go to hell."

Lewis's stare at Whitney could have frozen hot coffee. "You're thinking you'll work something out with the Feds, but I'm going to make sure that *doesn't* happen. One of your victims is in the hospital at this moment, fighting for her life. Now it's your turn."

"You just tryin' to trick me into talkin' to you," Whitney snorted.

Lewis wagged his head, mocking Whitney. "You *can't* make a deal with me. I don't *want* a deal with you. You're lucky to be above ground, Whitney. Remember your buddy, Tyrone? Tyrone Guyon? The Bellevue cops gunned him and his woman down as they were on their way to buy from you. They were in a Ford Maverick, not the white Lincoln. You'll be able to watch it on the evening news from your jail cell."

Whitney stared at Lewis, dumbfounded.

"Surprised? I'm putting out the word that *you* snitched Guyon off to Bellevue."

Whitney glared at Lewis. "You framin' me? I can get you, pig, from prison!"

Lewis shook his head dismissively. "Too late. I *already* set you up. When your customers don't see you're in the same slammer as them, it'll confirm what they're already thinking, that *you* set them up. We're putting you in a different jail."

Whitney was seething. Lewis continued.

Lewis handed Whitney to the additional patrol officers waiting outside. "Take him to our jail in a separate car. Book him into in the protective custody wing. *Then* transfer him to King County after two days. Tell them to put him in the protective custody wing there too."

When Whitney overheard Lewis's instructions, he screamed curses and threats and the officers had to fight him into the back of their cruiser.

AT THE INTENSIVE Care Unit of Overlake Hospital, Linda Ogilvie's parents and her brother stood beside her as she breathed her last. Hours earlier Linda had awakened long enough to ask God and her parents for forgiveness and to pray together, holding hands as a family for the final time. As they did, the nurse bolted out of the room in tears she could not hold back.

CHAPTER TWELVE
What's Past Is Prologue

MYRNA HITCHCOCK CLUNG to her only son's arm as she and her daughter Jean crossed the polished brown slate floor of The Barb restaurant. The hostess led them to a booth with cushy brown padded leather seats.

After the waitress brought menus, Myrna unloaded, "Roger, why didn't you at least *call* to tell me you're safe? Why did you let me worry like that!"

"Yeah, Roger," Jean chided, "learning about it on TV and not being able to reach you, Mom almost had a heart attack."

"I'm sorry for being so thoughtless. It happened late at night, and I didn't get to go home until daylight. By then I was too tired to think."

Myrna broke into tears. She daubed her eyes with a handkerchief. "I worried over your father coming back alive from the war in Europe," she sniffled. "Then I worried about you in Vietnam. My only son! You're

JOHN HANSEN

supposed to be safe now that you're home, but oh-no, you went from being a soldier to being a policeman. And in times like these! Now every time I hear sirens at night my heart races with fear. *Please* quit this cop business, and go back to medical school!"

Hitchcock held his silence, knowing his mother had more to say.

"Son, quit while you're still young and alive. The GI Bill will pay your tuition and help with the cost of your books. You'll make a fine doctor, like your dad."

"But, Mom–"

"And," she said, shaking her finger at him, "the Chatterton girl is right for you. She's very attracted to you, I could tell. If her inconsiderate, turncoat father hadn't been there, you two would be dating by now."

"Hold on, Mom–"

"I want you to give Emily another chance," Myrna insisted.

"Mom, your fixation with the Chatterton girl intrigues me. What is it about her you like so much?"

They paused in their conversation when the waitress brought coffee and took their orders.

"Emily hasn't been sleeping around like other girls her age," Myrna stated with an emphatic nod. "And she's a serving type who will take care of you, and you can trust her. And did you check out how she's built?"

"Uhh, no–not really, Mom."

"Oh shush!" Myrna said, digging her elbow into her

78

son. "Don't lie to me! You're my son! You're a man! A *real* man! *Of course,* you checked her out, I was watching you! She is *built* for popping out babies! *Big* babies can zip right through those broad hips without strain or harm. Her bosom isn't much to write home about, but a couple pregnancies will solve that problem to your liking."

Hitchcock inwardly shook his head as his mother went on.

"And, Roger, think about this: You are the end of the Hitchcock family line if you don't get busy and start having sons!"

"Will you be booking our wedding date and honeymoon plans too, Mom?" he teased.

Customers sitting close by listened to Myrna with amusement on their faces. He couldn't help laughing out loud, and Jean nearly fell out of the booth, laughing so hard she held her sides with both hands.

"Stop with the teasing you two," Myrna said, flapping up her linen napkin in a show of irritation. "I'm serious."

"We don't doubt that, Mom. Wow!" Jean chimed in.

"Mom," Hitchcock said, struggling to not smile, "are you really willing to risk having grandsons who resemble Emily's father...what's his name, Heath? Yeah, Heath. Bow ties, bushy eyebrows and all? Somebody should tell him the Groucho Marx look is out."

Jean burst into laughter again, laying on her side,

slapping the table with her hand. "Good one, Roger! Good one!"

Myrna ignored them, shaking her head in dismay. "This is what I get from my children after all my sacrifices. Like Rodney Dangerfield on TV, 'I get no respect,'" she muttered as she paid the bill.

† † †

A COLD WIND whipped Hitchcock's pant legs the next morning as he walked up to the granite headstone marked:

THEODORE IAN HITCHCOCK, M.D.
BELOVED HUSBAND, FATHER, SOLDIER
AND HEALER
1913-1966

Countless father-son talks came to mind as he faced the headstone. His dad's mentoring him into the code of championship—personal discipline, honor, protecting the weak burned into him from years of boxing, baseball and hard labor summer jobs. *"There is dignity in every job, Roger, no matter how lowly. And always remember, it is the duty of the strong to protect the weak,"* his dad taught him.

After his father passed, his experiences with death and dying during his Army years led him to doubt the existence of an afterlife. Because of his doubts, he struggled with the notion of talking to a hunk of stone. But there was the nagging possibility of more going on than what he knew from his five physical senses.

The granite headstone seemed to become a conduit to his father as he dropped to one knee. "I'm here, Dad," he said aloud. *Am I really talking to you or to a stone? Or just the bones under the stone? Or are you able to hear me even though you are in another realm? Doesn't make any difference, I guess, I'm here.*

"I'm following your example in everything but one thing, Dad, and I don't know if that will ever happen to me as it did to you. If you can see or hear me from where you are, you know how much I miss you. If only we could *really* talk. But this is all I have of you for now... I'm taking care of Mom and the girls. Joan and Darren have another baby on the way. Jean and I are still single," he said, having decided his father probably was listening.

"Things turned out as you said they would with Ruby, Dad. She became a different kind of woman while I was away, and I let her go."

He paused again.

"I had to kill a man the other day, Dad, a bad man who tried to kill me and my partner in an ambush. After it ended, I wondered if you or an angel had been there to protect us..."

Suddenly remembering the warning he received at the detective meeting, Hitchcock paused to look around to see if anyone was watching him. No one was, so he went on.

"I'm at a fork in the road with my life, now. Mom

wants me to quit police work and go back to medical school. I can't decide. They gave me some paid time off after the shooting, but there will be a formal review, like a trial, I guess. Before that happens, I need to get away for a while. Don't know where, just getting away is what matters."

As he turned to leave, he briefly touched the headstone with his right hand, and his eyes misted.

† † †

AN INTENSE SWIRL of longing and anger filled Gayle Warren, code-named Mata Hari, as she gazed with longing at the black-and-white snapshot in a dark wood frame on her nightstand, the only photograph of her family she had.

Her father, an ex-Marine, so young, strong and handsome, and her mother, petite and pretty. Her brother Tony wore a Roy Rogers cowboy hat and a cap gun in his holster and she, her hair in braids, clutched her only doll. A typical Tacoma working-class family, they were; poor, but loving and happy.

Burned into her soul was the night she learned a drunk driver crossed the center line, killing her parents. Their aged grandmother, though in failing health, stepped up to the plate, but died four years later, leaving her and Tony to fend for themselves. Gayle worked at different jobs to provide for Tony and herself, but without an authority figure to tell him what to do, Tony drifted into trouble, and drugs.

Then out of the blue came Rulee, a Creole man from Louisiana. His strikingly dark, handsome looks, warm personality and charming French Quarter drawl concealed the brutal enslaver of women he was. Young and vulnerable, Gayle fell for his flattering tongue and believed his endless lies. When brother Tony, by now a hardened user of whatever drugs he could get, moved into a rental house on Tacoma's Hilltop neighborhood with Rulee and the three young women in his harem, Gayle soon followed.

In a matter of weeks, Gayle's addiction to heroin led her to quit her sales position at the downtown JC Penney store. She became a full-time prostitute, like the other three girls, under Rulee. Then, when one of the other girls vanished, Gayle escaped.

† † †

HITCHCOCK'S PHONE RANG. A Records clerk relayed a request for him to call Aubrey Aramaki. He remembered Aubrey as a childhood friend from first grade through their senior year. Hitchcock recalled him as smart, handsome, friendly and generous, the kid everyone liked.

They met at Speed's Café, a checkerboard linoleum floor diner in the Lake Hills neighborhood shopping center. The place was quiet and the Greek couple who owned it were preparing for the dinner crowd.

"You look the same as when we graduated," Hitchcock said after the waitress poured their coffees.

Aubrey flashed his signature smile. "Yes, and life is good and still adventurous for you as well. I have been reading about you in the paper since my discharge. Congratulations on your victorious outcome with those two who ambushed you and your partner."

"Thanks."

"How interesting that we both served as soldiers in Vietnam," Aubrey said.

"When were you there and what did you do?"

"First Air Cavalry, Military Intelligence unit, stationed in Vietnam from 1968-1969," Aubrey said.

"Sounds James Bond-ish," Hitchcock said with admiration and keen interest.

"It really was. I remember one memorable situation where a sixteen-year-old prisoner knew the location of a cache of artillery weapons, and the location of his unit, but the assigned interrogation team got nothing out of him. My assignment was to make him talk."

"What did you do?"

"I gargled Johnny Walker scotch whiskey and entered the tent where the prisoner was being held. With alcohol on my breath, I jumped on the prisoner, grabbed his throat with one hand, pulled out my 45 caliber from my shoulder holster with my other hand, pointed it between his eyes and yelled and screamed obscenities, which of course he didn't understand, until my interpreter grabbed me from behind and told the prisoner, 'This American hates Vietnamese and would love to just shoot you.'"

"And then?"

Aubrey chuckled. "And then the prisoner told me where they hid the cache and the position of his unit. I received a bronze star for that mission, although my only intention for such a Hollywood maneuver was not to harm the prisoner but to save him and save American lives."

"You did us proud."

"I excelled at intelligence work. Not only at going undercover to collect information, but also in analyzing it. Hated leaving it when I was discharged."

"Maybe I should call you 007 from now on."

Aubrey laughed.

"What's next for you?"

"I'm headed to Japan, the birthplace of my parents. I want to learn the language of my ancestors."

"We've known each other since elementary school, but I never knew. Your parents... Did the government...?"

"Yes," Aubrey said, still smiling, finishing the awkward sentence for him. "The government took my father and mother from their home and shipped them in a cattle car to a concentration camp in Tule Lake in California during the war. My father was born in Bellevue in 1913, on 116th, where Auto Row is now. In spite of the injustice done to my family, a couple of my uncles joined the Army and became part of the famous 442nd Infantry, the Japanese unit that fought with distinction in Europe."

Bitter empathy flooded Hitchcock. "They lost their property, didn't they?"

"Yes," Aubrey replied without a hint of anger.

His calm forgiveness humbled Hitchcock. "Since much of the internment camp was economically motivated," he went on, "the only way the Japanese Americans would lose their properties would be if they didn't pay property taxes. They had no income or communication available to them so their properties went out to auction."

Red-faced with shame and anger, Hitchcock blurted, "That's horrible! The government treated your parents and your uncles like enemies, seized their property illegally, yet they still volunteered to fight for the country of their choice. *I* feel guilty and I wasn't even born yet!"

"But wait, Roger," Aubrey said, holding up his hand. "Some good did happen for a few. I believe my uncle Min is one, but I'm not entirely sure. While shopping in downtown Bellevue after the repatriation, he ran into the person who 'acquired' his house in Bellevue. He asked Min where he had been and said he had been waiting for him to return. Min assumed he had lost his house like most of the other Nisei's did, but this man said 'I have been waiting for your return. We rented the house and even put in a bathroom in it. The house is ready for you.' This actually happened to my parents also."

Moved to tears he couldn't hide, Hitchcock got up. He gave Aubrey a hearty handshake and clapped him on the arm.

"We have more in common than our childhoods, Roger," Aubrey said.

"Like what?" Hitchcock asked as he wiped his tears.

"We both have long shadows over us."

"What do you mean?"

"Your dad served in the Army during World War II, as a medic, like you did in Vietnam."

"Yes, and his father, my granddad, did the same in the First World War," Hitchcock said.

"I also served in wartime, like my uncles did, and you. Don't you see?"

Hitchcock shrugged. "See what?"

"The past governs the present and the future to an unknown degree. By volunteering to serve in the military in a time of war, we followed the footsteps of our immediate ancestors. Their shadows guide us. We will guide those who come after us."

Aubrey's words penetrated Hitchcock. He nodded his head in understanding. "I think you've got something there. More than you realize, Aubrey."

"Police work has always interested me," Aubrey

went on. "When I came home, the Seattle Police offered me a job straight into detectives because of my military background and my heritage. I declined because I want to pursue certain business interests in Japan and other places."

After a pause, Aubrey continued. "I also thought it wouldn't be fair to uniformed officers who hoped for a chance to make detective. Every man has a duty to pay his dues."

"Right again, Aubrey," Hitchcock said, admiring his friend's integrity.

"Now that we met again, Roger, and I have read about what you are doing, I may be able to help you in your work."

"Like how?"

"Now is not the time. When I have something of value to give you, you will hear from 007, that will be my code name."

"Okay. But now I get it," Hitchcock said.

"How's that, Roger?"

"No matter which generation we look at, what's past is prologue."

"Yes! Next time we meet, we'll drink to it. Whiskey, of course," Hitchcock said.

Aubrey flashed that smile again. "Yes! Johnny Walker scotch!"

CHAPTER THIRTEEN
In Re Justice

FROM SPEED'S CAFE Hitchcock drove to Gayle's apartment. Desire for her flooded him when she opened her door, looking luscious in a simple white T-shirt and jeans.

"Hi. You saved my life and—" She wrapped her arms around him before he finished, pressing herself into him. "My heart almost stops when I think about Guyon trying to kill you," she said, weeping. She took a step back and wiped her eyes. "But I have to confess...I also did this to even a score."

"Score?"

"Bad memories returned the only time Guyon came to The Wagon Wheel. I knew him for what he was—a pimp—and I hated him. Our redneck customers bullied him until he left, and I was glad."

"I'm sorry for the loss of your brother. Too often life is hard and unfair," he sympathized.

"In a way, my brother Tony's murder is avenged

now."

He put his hands upon her shoulders. "What's this? Your brother was murdered?"

She sniffed as she nodded. "A pusher named Rulee got me high on heroin. I was already hooked but he gave me more than usual so I wouldn't interfere when I saw what he would do next."

"What happened next?"

"We were in an abandoned apartment building. He forced me to watch him murder Tony by overdose. He broke me by taking the only family I had left, so I had no one to stop from owning me. Guyon was like Rulee, a slave master. He and that evil Mae Driscoll didn't deserve to live."

He handed her an envelope. She pushed his hand away.

"I don't want money for this."

"Take it. I passed the collection plate. Everybody chipped in."

She put the envelope in her pocket. "The other guy you're looking for at the Hilltop, Ronald Davis, tall skinny black guy, drives a Caddy?"

"Tell me more," he nodded.

"He took over Guyon's territory, including the Hilltop, right after you killed Guyon. The word in Seattle's Central District is the Bellevue cops, meaning you, executed them because Guyon was black and Mae was white. Davis is scared of Bellevue cops now, especially you. Word is that the Hilltop crowd thinks you're trigger-happy. Watch your back, Roger. Everyone in Eastgate knows who you are."

"Noted."

She put her hand on his chest, looked up at him and said, "I want to keep doing this work. For my parents, my brother, and my grandmother."

He gently laid his hand over hers. "You understand you could be hurt or killed," he said. "These people think of killing someone like we think of going to a movie."

"I have another reason for taking these risks," she said.

"What is it?"

She pressed her head into his chest. "Not now," she whispered.

† † †

AFTER MANY ARRESTS for drug possession and use, underage drinking, bar fights, an avalanche of citizen and police complaints finally motivated the City Attorney's office to file charges against The Trunk Lid, Bellevue's first infamous bar. The first cases involving appeared on the docket of the Bellevue Municipal Court.

First up, eighteen-year-old Barry Walters appeared with his dad and dad's high-priced attorney. The City Attorney's Office turned to their toughest prosecutor, Eve Claussen.

The biggest challenge Claussen faced wasn't the

defense attorney, but the judge, Malcom Hadley, the Bellevue court's only judge.

Judge Hadley's leniency stemmed not from a liberal political outlook, but from a strict Mennonite up-bringing, which resulted in a sheltered childhood. An only child, Hadley's parents were people of the soil, orchardists, in rural Eastern Washington. Malcolm's lips never met a girl's lips until he married. He was a lifetime stranger to tobacco, drugs and alcohol.

Not surprisingly, Judge Hadley's rulings often infuriated prosecutors, cops and victims by changing guilty pleas to "not guilty" without the defendants' request or permission, which were followed by lengthy philosophical monologues before he dismissed the charges, without hearing a word from the defendant.

Defense attorneys took ruthless advantage of Judge Hadley's inability to accept that human nature has a dark side which must be restrained. In keeping with their arrogance, over drinks in their favorite watering holes after trial, they mocked and mimicked Judge Hadley behind his back.

After studying the police reports, Eve called in Traffic Division Sergeant Bill Harris as a rebuttal witness. Harris would testify that he was at The Trunk Lid off duty with three other off-duty officers, when they witnessed the entire attack on Officer Forbes and intervened on Forbes's behalf.

Barry's defense attorney, eager to rack up fees by

going to trial, declined the City's settlement offers.

"How does the defendant plead?" asked Judge Hadley.

"The defendant pleads 'not guilty' on all four charges, Your Honor, and is ready to proceed," crowed the cocky defense attorney, Mr. Cheatham.

Judge Hadley peered over his spectacles at Cheatham. "You seem familiar to me, Counselor."

Cheatham stood and flashed a smiled beneath his new Hawaiian suntan. "I haven't appeared before Your Honor for some time. I am Will Cheatham. My firm recently merged with two others. We are in business now as Duey, Cheatham and Howe."

"Hmm, Do we, cheat 'em and how, hmm," Judge Hadley repeated with a quick grin. "Has quite a witty ring to it. But, let's proceed."

"The City of Bellevue calls Officer Mark Forbes to the stand," the prosecutor, Eve Claussen said.

After Forbes's testimony for the prosecution, Will Cheatham grilled Forbes ruthlessly, skillfully luring him into an open display of anger. Those in the courtroom snickered at Forbes' loss of composure. Forbes blushed from embarrassment. Barry and his father snickered at him as he stepped down.

"The City calls Sergeant Bill Harris to the stand," the prosecutor said.

"Objection, Your Honor. The City didn't give adequate notice to defense counsel of its intent to call this witness," Mr. Cheatham said, not standing before he addressed the judge.

Judge Hadley shifted his eyes to the prosecutor, who got to her feet. "Your Honor, the City notified defense counsel by certified mail of our intention to call Sergeant Harris and copies of his report six weeks ago. I am ready to submit the certified mail receipts, if Your Honor requires," Claussen countered.

As Sergeant Harris testified regarding the attack on Forbes by the defendant and his friends, Judge Hadley, raised to be a pacifist, suddenly remembered his parents' teaching of the Bible verse in the Book of Romans: *The officer is an agent of God's wrath to bring punishment on the wrongdoer. He does not bear the sword for nothing.* His Uncle Matthias, his father's brother, came to mind. As the Undersheriff of the county for many years, he single-handedly tracked down and subdued many hardened criminals to bring them to justice. The Judge flashed back to his youth, sitting in his uncle's patrol car, a late '40s Ford, listening to the police radio.

"Stop, Sergeant," Judge Hadley interrupted, to everyone's surprise. "You may step down, I've heard enough."

"In that case, the defense rests. Thank you, Your Honor." Mr. Cheatham smirked, winking at his client.

The surprised prosecutor stood. "With no other choice, the City rests, Your Honor," she said, disappointment in her voice.

Sergeant Bill Harris stepped down, his face red with visible anger and embarrassment.

"The defendant will step forward to the bench for a word with me before I render my decision," Judge Hadley said.

Barry's father snickered as Barry swaggered up to the Judge's bench, grinning, and leaned on the podium with his elbow.

"Yeah?" he said, staring at the Judge, his mouth hanging open in a mocking manner.

For the first time in anyone's memory, Judge Hadley's face darkened. "I find you guilty of all four charges," he said. "Stand back while I render your sentences."

Barry stepped back slowly, shocked.

Judge Hadley turned to his clerk. "Get me two officers. Now."

When two uniformed officers entered the courtroom and acknowledged the Judge with a nod, the spoiled young punk began shaking. Judge Hadley stared down at Barry, his eyes filled with righteous indignation.

"Young man," Judge Hadley said. "I find you guilty of being a Minor in Possession of alcohol, for which you will serve thirty days in the county jail."

Bang went the gavel.

"You can't do that!" Barry's father shouted, jumping to his feet.

"Your Honor!" Mr. Cheatham blurted as he jumped to his feet. "This is extreme!"

Judge Hadley scowled down at Mr. Cheatham. "Attacking a police officer *is* what's extreme, Counselor. And a *grave* offense against the community. You will *restrain* your client. One more outburst from him and I will jail him for Contempt of Court."

Barry shot a fearful glance over his shoulder at the two uniformed officers. There would be no escape. He started to cry. "Help me, Dad! You told me this would be a piece of cake!"

That last remark brought a scowl to Judge Hadley's face. Grimly he continued. "On the charge of Resisting Arrest," he said, staring hard at Barry's father. "I find you guilty, for which you will serve thirty days in the county jail."

Bang went the gavel again.

A hush fell over the courtroom. Barry's shoulders slumped when he saw the uniformed policemen position themselves on either side, within arms' reach of him.

"On the charge of Assaulting a Police Officer, I find you guilty and sentence you to *sixty* days in the county jail."

Bang went the gavel again.

Mr. Cheatham put his hand on the arm of Barry's father and leaned toward him as he said, "Don't worry. This is just part of the show. He'll suspend everything after this last charge and give Barry probation."

Judge Hadley overheard Cheatham's remark. Staring at Cheatham, the judge continued. "For the final charge of Attempted Escape, I find you guilty and sentence you to thirty days in the county jail." The gavel fell a final time.

"Officers, take custody of this defendant and book him at once into the King County Jail. The clerk will have the forms ready as you leave."

Cheatham slammed his pencil upon the table, rolled his eyes and let out a loud groan. The prosecutor and Forbes stared at each other, too stunned to speak.

Barry broke into sobbing as handcuffs clicked on his wrists. His father seized Mr. Cheatham by the sleeve of his silk suit jacket.

"Do something, Cheatham, damn you!"

Will Cheatham jumped to his feet, his face ashen, voice stammering. "Y-your Honor! Am I–may I...I assume these sentences are to run concurrently?"

Judge Hadley glared at Cheatham. "The sentences will run *consecutively*, counselor." Cheatham gripped the edge of the counsel table, almost fainting. He gazed at the table, feeling his client's rage without looking at him. He felt humiliated, losing a case so badly in front of the judge the defense attorneys in town loved to mock and mimic over drinks.

The court clerk grinned as she noted the sentences. The station officers led Barry, sniveling, out of the courtroom. Desperate, Cheatham tried one last objection.

"But Your Honor, that means this poor boy will spend a hundred fifty days in jail. Six months!"

Judge Hadley's eyes bore holes into Cheatham. "Even your math is off, Counselor. One-hundred-fifty days is *five* months, not six. The clerk's office will hand you the defendant's papers on your way out. Call the next case."

Those inside the courtroom smiled and nodded at each other when they heard Barry's father in the hall, shouting curses at his attorney, refusing to pay his fees while Cheatham pleaded, saying "What could I do? The Judge threw us a curve."

DURING THE RECESS, Judge Hadley called Chief Carter from his chambers. "I normally don't stick my nose into your business, Sean," he said, "but I just had a case in which one of your boys got beat up by a bunch of drunken minors inside a bar called The Trunk Lid. What are you doing to shut that place down?"

"I'll get someone on it, Malcom. What did *you* do about it in court? Slap his wrist, give him one of your speeches?" Chief Carter replied sarcastically.

"Nope. Threw the young punk in jail for five months. Almost tossed his dad in the bucket too for contempt," the judge snorted. "Try showing some guts, sometime, Sean. It feels great."

CHAPTER FOURTEEN
Feminine Primal

HIS JANGLING PHONE roused Hitchcock out of a deep, dreamless sleep. He picked up the receiver, unable to say anything.

"Hi Roger. It's Eve. Can you meet me at The Barb for lunch today?"

Surprised, he rubbed his eyes and cleared his throat.

"What time?"

"Twelve-thirty?"

He glanced at his Timex. 11:07. "I'll be there."

After a quick run with Jamie on the wooded trails and gravel roads of Wilburton Hill, he came back refreshed, his lungs filled with the cool, moist air of the Northwest. Wondering why the urgent tone in Eve's voice, he knocked out three sets of pushups, fifty reps each, sixty seconds apart. He stretched his muscles and tendons, showered, shaved and dressed in laundered jeans, a tan cotton shirt, black gabardine sport jacket, brown loafers.

He arrived at The Barb at 12:10, early enough, he thought, to watch Eve enter the restaurant.

"Officer Hitchcock?" asked the young receptionist wearing a white chiffon blouse with pearl earrings, matching necklace and black skirt. He nodded, wondering how she recognized him. She took two menus and said, "Follow me, please."

He followed her through The Barb's Western motif, the polished brown slate floor and wood-paneled walls, past the dining room lined with posh leather booths and scenes of ranch roundups, the less formal lunch counter with swivel chairs mounted to the floor and rustic booths along the opposite wall.

Four private dining rooms were on the right side of the corridor that ended at the cocktail lounge, where the smells of bourbon and the sounds of customers and the clinking of ice and glass met him.

At the last and smallest private meeting room, the receptionist smiled as she opened the door where Eve stood at attention, waiting at the only table, a beaming smile on her face.

† † †

A STRANGE BLOOD-rush coursed through Eve the second Hitchcock appeared. She didn't recognize it for what it was—an ancient, primal stirring, long buried under generations of civilized living. She ran her hands over his arms and shoulders, then buried her head into his chest, her body shaking with primal desire as she held him tightly.

"I'm so glad you won," she whispered with awe.

Feeling awkward under such an intense spotlight of admiration, he said nothing.

"The whole thing is a miracle," Eve, the classic Scandinavian beauty told him in a guttural tone of voice as she continued pressing herself into him.

He took a half-step back to look at her. Almost six feet tall, curly blonde locks, fair skin, chiseled features with a svelte figure. He moved a chair to the other side of the table so he would sit facing the door. Without a word she moved her chair next to his, hip-to-hip, her deep-set blue eyes looking at him with wonderment. All he could do was grin sheepishly.

He admired Eve's cosmopolitanism and striking appearance. Combined with her keen intellect, she made for a formidable courtroom presence. She won many of the weakest cases for the City, especially in jury trials. He had heard that defense attorneys dreaded going against her because of her conviction record and aggressive pushing for jail time, which made her the cops' favorite.

Her visceral response to his role in deadly close-quarter combat surprised—and disturbed him. He saw the she-wolf in her, lusting for a taste of killing, vicariously through him, relishing risk and danger.

"I read your report, and Tom Sherman's too. I can't *imagine* being in danger like that! Tell me every detail—I want to know," she gushed. "What went through your mind—your emotions? Weren't you scared? You had to be."

He disliked talking about deadly combat as a form of amusement, but Eve was a key part of his informant network. Through her he knew what no one else on at his level on the Department knew about the secret doings of a clandestine group in city management and that they were connected to groups outside the city. She hadn't named anyone, but what she did tell him was enough to save his career just a few months ago. He couldn't afford to alienate or disappoint her. After the waitress left with their order, her eyes glistened as he began.

"A sort of slow-motion tunnel vision takes over when you realize your life could end in the next second," he said, "your mind and body downshift into survival mode. Your performance falls to the lowest level of your training."

Eve smoothed her napkin on her lap. She looked into his eyes. "I'm not following you. Please explain."

"The body can be trained to keep going when stress makes the brain go into neutral," he said, looking at her.

"Like cruise control?"

"Sort of. In boxing we trained so much that when exhaustion and pain reached a certain point, the brain would shift into neutral while the body kept up the fight automatically. So, when the shooting started, my brain went into neutral and my training and experience took over. I practice with my weapon almost daily, so I didn't have to think. I automatically drew and started shooting."

"That is why I remembered almost nothing right afterward, even how many shots I fired. The details sort of trickle back in," he added.

She stared at him, speechless.

"You and Tom Sherman are combat veterans, right?" she asked. "You guys won because you had been through this before, right?"

"I shouldn't say more before the inquest."

She ran her fingers through his close-cut dark brown hair. "Of course, but do tell me later."

"My turn," he said. "Why did you risk everything you've worked for to warn me about Bostwick?"

The waitress brought their orders, a Waldorf salad for her, prime rib dip with au jus for him, no fries, coffee for both. Hitchcock was hungry. They ate in silence at first, then she exhaled, paused and looked at Hitchcock.

"During the fifties, the time of my childhood, my dad was the police chief in a small town in California," she said.

He stopped eating and looked at her. "Your father was a cop?"

"Dad stumbled onto something that got him

JOHN HANSEN

entangled in a dispute with the town's rich and powerful" she replied. "He was the kind of man who always did the right thing, no matter what. He went on a call one day, and didn't come back. A couple days later they found him in his police car on a rural dirt road, shot in the head."

Tears formed in her eyes. She stopped talking, her head drooped.

He put his hand on her shoulder. She put her hand on his and held it. After a moment she took a breath and went on. "No investigation. Nothing was ever done. My dad was buried as if he had died of natural causes. A police chief, murdered, no action taken."

"What did your mother do?"

"She asked around, but no one would answer her questions."

"What about going to the press?" he asked.

"The local paper was owned by a town councilman," she said. "Years later, after I passed the California bar exam, I tried to get the FBI to look into what happened to my dad. No response. I hired a private investigator who was a retired FBI agent. He was only able to learn that my dad discovered something the powers-that-be who ran the town were involved in. They couldn't convince my dad to keep quiet once he found out about it."

"Did you ever learn what it was that they were willing to kill for?" he asked gently.

Eve lapsed into silence before she continued. "No. To this day I'm *still* his little girl," she said, emotion choking her voice.

Hitchcock sensed she had more to say. He held his silence, pushing the remains of his sandwich around with his fork, waiting.

"History repeats itself, Roger."

"It does," he agreed.

"Where I work, I see the same trends developing that led to my father's murder and the coverup."

He frowned, took a sip of coffee. "Explain."

"Big-money people from out of state are quietly moving in, influencing changes in the makeup of local government," she said, her eyes fixed on his. "Their kind hates incorruptible people, like my dad, like you, and I hate them. I was too young to help my dad, but now I have a chance to protect another incorruptible man and vindicate my father by protecting you from enemies you can't see."

Eve turned in her chair so that her knees touched his. "My other reason is our relationship. I want to keep it and protect it as long as possible."

"I'm sorry about your father. I would have liked to meet him, go on patrol with him."

"Thank you," she nodded. "You and Dad would have made a great team. Now listen to my words—I hear your name often mentioned as the main one, but not the only, officer certain people *in* the City and *not* in the City say in closed door meetings they want to be rid of."

Hitchcock shifted in his seat, dismayed. "Why?"

"You stand out too much. You're local, a boxing champ, a war hero, you make headlines with your police work almost every time you go on duty. You're serious about your work. Your dad was one of the town fathers and an icon. You're winning the public. As chief you'd be unstoppable. The snakes upstairs know they wouldn't be able to control you."

He took a deep breath. As he exhaled, he looked at Eve and shifted in his chair again. "I'm doing exactly what I want to do. Becoming chief never entered my mind. Whoever *they* are can relax."

"*None* of 'em are gonna believe that," she snorted.

He took another sip of his coffee and stared ahead. "And I'm not a war hero."

"Come *on*," she scoffed. "I've read your file. As a member of the City Attorney's office, I've been to meetings where I heard key people say those very things. They know all about you. Decorated for bravery, you saved the lives of your fellow soldiers and Vietnamese villagers on your first tour and your second tour is classified; for a reason, no doubt."

Hitchcock shrugged and said nothing.

The waitress returned. Eve ordered a slice of German chocolate cake and coffee for dessert. He ordered apple pie.

"They're using Bostwick to keep new officers of

your type out by failing them on their probation" Eve said after the waitress left and their table was bussed. "They were very displeased with him when you passed your probationary review. He's been on shaky ground with them since then and he blames you for it. He's bitter and vindictive. Never let your guard down."

He nodded. "Thanks to you, I not only survived his attack, I turned the tables on him. But what is this hush-hush all about?"

Eve paused as the desserts were brought. When the waitress left, she continued. "It would be unwise if I told you everything now. Later, maybe."

He stared at her, waiting.

"Okay," she said, "only this. Their goals are large-scale and long-term. The stakes are high and they don't want proactive policemen like you and certain others on the force who would expose them if they found out what they're really up to. They only want a token agency that writes traffic tickets, investigates accidents and visits kids in the schools. Officer Friendly stuff."

His coffee had grown cold. He shifted in his seat. "How does Bostwick fit into this?" he asked.

"Rowland Bostwick is their boy," Eve said. "His family came here three years ago from the East Coast with deep political connections and wealth going back generations. The plan is to make Bostwick the next chief because he'll do what they want, and his family's connections to powerful people on the East Coast are key to their goals of consolidation of power and control."

"Who exactly is involved?"

Eve shook her head. "You're safer if I don't tell you. Maybe later."

"Safer?" he echoed. "Safer from what? Who? Exactly what is the danger? I don't see anything except a bad joke named Bostwick."

She touched his arm for emphasis. "Wake *up*! You, and certain others are at risk, not only your careers, but possibly your lives. Your close friend Joel Otis is another officer they've got their sights on."

Stunned, he said "Otis?" He sat back, staring at her. "Okay," he said after long seconds. "Now I get it. His family was among the founders here, as mine was. Our military paths are almost identical."

"Finally, you see a little of the light, Good!" Eve said. "At the moment you, more than anyone, worry them. You have a bull's eye on your back."

"Thanks for the warning. I owe you one." He checked his Timex. "Say, aren't you due back at the office?"

Eve smiled and put her hand on his. "I have the rest of the day off, and yes, you owe me one, and I want to collect. My place—now."

HE RETURNED HOME near midnight and built a fire instead of turning in. As he sat with a cup of reheated coffee, doctored with half-and-half and honey, Jamie at his side, watching orange flames licking the logs, listening to police sirens in the distance, he thought about his relationship with Eve.

It began as a strong case of physical attraction. *Is it love?* he asked himself. *Not for me. For her? Possibly. After today I know Eve isn't informing on city officials and their clients for me per se. Her quest is to satisfy a long-hidden agenda centered around her father's murder. Eve did me a favor by warning me of my status as a political target. But because she wants no reward for her information, she holds the upper hand in our relationship, which puts me on thin ice.*

GAYLE WARREN RETURNED home after helping close The Wagon Wheel at 2:00 a.m. Two men asked her out during her shift, but she turned them down. She would let nothing interfere with her pursuit of Hitchcock, and she was still basking in the satisfaction of the role she played in putting an end to Tyrone Guyon and Mae Driscoll.

Their deaths made her feel almost vindicated from her past in Tacoma, but once Rulee realized that she saw him take the life of the other girl, Marie, he would set out to find and silence her. Now that she had Hitchcock in her life, if she played her cards right, Rulee, too, is a dead man.

Her hopes to be Hitchcock's woman were revived

when she realized how pleased he was with her work. The huge risks to her safety she took weren't for the money, though it helped. Spying for Hitchcock and turning down the many date offers she got afforded her the chance to be near him regularly.

Of the many men she had known, Hitchcock was worth risking her life for, even dying for. Given her past as a heroin junkie, being his spy offered her only the slimmest chance for him. Would she lose him if he knew she had also been a prostitute? Probably he figured it out right away and said nothing. As a stained woman, she had to play her hand wisely. No room for mistakes. If she won him, she would be his and his alone. She would be safe even if Rulee found her. She would bear his children, keep her good figure, get her GED, learn to cook and keep house.

With gut-level love and hunger for a certain man driving her, Gayle set her sights on drug dealer Ronald Davis as her next target. She would keep going until she either landed the man of her dreams or died trying.

† † †

KAREN SHERMAN THOUGHT it strange how her husband's brushes with death sharpened her hunger for him, like falling in love with the man over and over again who seems indestructible, immortal. But this time she noticed a different aspect to her attraction to Tom that she didn't understand. It was an intense, primeval drive. As if a wild animal inside her emerged, driving her to him in ways beyond the torrid draw to him she felt on their honeymoon. The beast feline lusted to experience the thrill of coming through mortal danger through her man.

Her bond with Tom entered a new phase after the shooting disturbed her. She held him, not able to let him out of her sight, fearing he would disappear, never to return. She hated seeing him leave for work, wondering each time if this was the dreaded day he wouldn't make it back.

One side of Karen wanted Tom to find a safer, more normal line of work, but she couldn't tell him that. Not now. The other side, the rush she felt in his coming home victorious in dangerous situations, was becoming more dominant. It enhanced his appeal to her in ways she would lose if he left police work. Down deep, she feared she might be less attracted to him if he took a civilian job.

"When will they return your gun?" Karen asked.

Startled by her question, Sherman replied, "It might be a couple weeks. There's lab testing to be done to reconstruct the gunfight."

"You mean to know who shot who?" she asked as she ran her hands up over his shoulders.

"Yep," he answered, giving her a quick grin.

Karen inserted her fingers into his empty holster. "Didn't they give you a replacement gun?"

Surprised, Sherman answered "They will. Maybe tomorrow. What's with the interest in my gun, anyway?"

She hesitated before she said, "I'm still learning."

"What?" he asked, puzzled as he stroked her golden hair.

"That I'm safer when my man is armed," she said huskily.

When a sly smirk came over Sherman's face, Karen took hold of his uniform shirt. "Just lie next to me, now."

CHAPTER FIFTEEN
The Femme Fatale

IN HER CUSTOM-BUILT home on top of Cougar Mountain, between Bellevue and Issaquah, Juju Kwan slipped out of bed. It was the crack of dawn. She hurried to get her camera out, pulled the blanket off her sleeping conquest, took three pictures of him, replaced the covers and put the camera away.

She inspected herself in the full-length mirror inside her walk-in closet. At thirty-one, her beauty was as perfect and luscious as in her twenties. Everything was in the right place—her full, jet-black hair draped over her shoulders and down her back like fine silk, her taut, smooth, supple skin, flat stomach, a firm, full bosom and shapely legs.

For a war orphan who grew up in a brothel in Taiwan, she had come a long way in a man's world. Her beauty, coupled with the cunning and skills of her past, brought her to America, a remarkable feat, and even now, in her thirties, few men, young or old, could resist her sensual, exotic beauty.

The new worry lines she now saw on her forehead were caused, no doubt, by the pressure of Hitchcock's constant lurking about. She knew from her sources in the police that he used informants. His recent killing of Tyrone Guyon, one of her most regular customers, and the loss of a large cache of heroin that followed put her in the spotlight of her silent backers here and in Taiwan. She was under pressure to find out how Hitchcock knew to intercept and arrest hitman Colin Wilcox. Naturally, her bosses suspect a leak. She did too, but who?

Juju dared not tell anyone that she harbored a secret, fatal attraction to Hitchcock. She knew it wasn't mutual, that he had no use for her. She also knew that, if he didn't die first, he would be her undoing. Like a death wish, she wanted him anyway. After the deaths of Guyon and Mae Driscoll, Juju sensed that Death would be coming for either her or Hitchcock next. If only Hitchcock had died in the shoot-out instead of Guyon, the troubles plaguing her wouldn't exist and the dangerous change in tactics now in motion wouldn't be necessary.

She slipped into her silk robe, ran a brush through her hair and studied the sleeping man in her bed. Flabby and ugly, she struggled to even touch him, yet he was a valuable asset, but not her only one. She owned another man, placed even higher than this one. The one in her bed didn't yet realize the degree to which she owned him, body and soul. When the time is right, he will.

She paused, as she often did, to take in the breathtaking view of Lake Sammamish as she passed through the living room to the kitchen. And as she always, the view led her to marvel at the contrast between her humble beginnings as a Taipei prostitute and bar girl to where she is now.

In her new modern kitchen, Juju brewed his coffee his way—extra strong, heavy on the cream and sugar and returned to the bedroom. "Time get up! Mama-san make fresh coffee for papa-san!"

The man stirred slightly. The drug she'd slipped into his drink during the night was wearing off.

Juju shook him gently by the shoulder. "Time get up, Rowlie-san, Loo-tenahnt, sir!"

CHAPTER SIXTEEN
Jim Reynolds, and a Plot Exposed

HIS NIGHTSTAND CLOCK as he reached for his phone read a minute past seven. He recognized the caller's resonant baritone voice immediately.

"Good morning, Roger boy, Frank Kilmer here. I know you're on paid leave, but I developed the film you took from the private eye. Better get here quick. In an hour I'm leaving for a week."

He rubbed the sleep from his eyes. "You at the lab now?"

"Yep"

"Be there in twenty," he yawned.

The photo lab door was posted with the sign: DO NOT DISTURB. DARKROOM IN OPERATION when he arrived fifteen minutes later. He went in and rapped on the darkroom door.

"It's Roger, Frank."

"The manila envelope on my desk is for you."

He counted nineteen 4x6 color photographs of Allie's ex-husband coming and going from Allie's apartment, her two meetings at Ramona's Café with an unidentified man he assumed must be the mysterious Jim Reynolds, plus Allie's first meeting with him in his car behind the bank, and again at Nick's BBQ.

Somebody's got deep pockets to pay for all this. The private detective followed Allie for weeks, if not months, he concluded.

The last photograph brought a smile to his face. It showed the mystery man getting into an old gray Volvo sedan, the license plate was legible. Now he had something to go on.

† † †

TO HER SURPRISE, Allie lost sleep worrying about what would happen to Hitchcock after the shooting. Would relatives or friends of the people he killed be out to kill him in retaliation? Then there was the possibility the Department wouldn't back him. Then what? The intensity of her feelings when he didn't call as he promised surprised her.

Day after day she watched for him through the window of the Pancake Corral while she waited on customers. When he unexpectedly walked in and smiled at her, she blew up.

"Where have you been, ya big lug, and why didn't you call me like you said you would? I've been worried *sick* about you. Damn you!" she shouted.

The cooks behind the counter stopped cooking, the customers in the nearest booths stopped eating. Everyone stared in shock.

"May I sit down?" He asked, his tone gentle.

Ashamed of herself, tears filling her eyes, Allie gestured to an empty booth.

"Yes, of course. I'm sorry," she said, huskiness in her voice.

"No, *I* apologize, Allie. This has been a very big deal and the inquiry isn't over yet. Please forgive me. I was wrong to not call you back," he said tenderly.

She wanted to touch him, at least his hand, but the customers, both cooks, and the waitresses were watching. "Of course I forgive you," she whispered, her voice husky with emotion. "I'll get you some coffee."

"I have some photos to show you."

"I'm still working,"

"I'll wait all day if need be."

Allie managed a quick grin of hope and forgiveness and briefly touched his hand as she poured his coffee. "Buckwheats and bacon, comin' up," she said, just above a whisper.

THIRTY MINUTES LATER, when the last customers were gone, she came to his table. He gestured to the empty chair. "You'd better take a seat for this, Allie."

He showed her the photo of a man getting into his

car. "Is this the Jim Reynolds guy?"

"Yep. That's him."

"The car registration and the photograph I'm about to show you proves he isn't Jim Reynolds."

She gasped when he showed her a prison mugshot of the same man, his real name of BRUCE SANDS posted at the bottom.

"Bruce Sands is a bank robber recently released from McNeil Island."

She stared at the mugshot in disbelief. "What's McNeil Island?"

"A federal prison in Puget Sound, near Olympia. Sands has more than bank robbery on his record, and he's a radical."

Her face blanched. "I'm scared, Roger. What now?"

"The private investigator I caught photographing you wouldn't say who his client is."

"It can't be anyone but Horace MacAuliffe, my ex-father-in-law. He tried to get custody of Trevor from me a year ago. I thought with all his power and money he would win, but to my surprise the judge ruled in my favor. I never hear from them anymore."

"Wrong. You've been hearing from them all along through their private investigator and this guy Sands. And you will again, after they're done paying others to frame you as an unfit parent."

"Now what, Roger? I'm broke."

He smiled. "I have a plan."

.

CHAPTER SEVENTEEN
A High-Country Hiatus

GLOOMY WEATHER, UNENDING controversy over the shooting, an inquest hanging over his head, swirling departmental rumors and petty politics brought him to the edge of burnout. He needed a break to survive. But where to go in the winter?

"Open spaces, horses, outdoor work and home cooking are what you need," Rhonda told him. "My family's ranch has all that. I have time off coming to me. We'll need my four-wheel-drive to get through the snow and ice at the Pass. Bring warm work clothes, gloves, boots, hat and a rifle if you have one. We'll split the driving."

He rode in silence, Rhonda driving, Jamie lying on a blanket covering the back seat. They crested the snowy ski slopes of Snoqualmie Pass. His mood brightened when the sun came out, the sky changed from the low gray clouds of Seattle to the sunny, frigid blue skies of

Eastern Washington. He turned the radio on. "Find some country music," he said, looking happily at Rhonda.

"Did you know how much you helped the girl who survived the shooting, Linda Ogilvie?" she asked him.

He glanced at her. "I heard she didn't make it," he said.

"She didn't."

"So how did I help her?"

"Stopping her bleeding gave her a few more days. She gave the detective information and reconciled with her parents. The nurse told me she passed peacefully."

"How did you know it was me who patched her up at the scene?"

"The officer who arrived with her to collect evidence–LaPerle."

He smiled as he looked out the window. "We call him Frenchie."

"Yeah? As bad as her condition was, she was cute."

He shook his head. "Pitiful. Because of heroin she was a slave to Guyon. She was three years behind me at Sammamish High."

"Dr. Townsend, her physician, was curious to know if the information she gave to the detective just before she died was of any help."

He poured coffee from a thermos. "I've been told the Seattle narcs made a large seizure of heroin and cocaine and made several arrests based on Linda's information."

Rhonda nodded, keeping her hands on the wheel and her eyes on the road as the Suburban slipped slightly on patches of hard-packed ice. They were passing ski lodges at the summit when she said "I was impressed by the wound dressing for Linda you did under adverse conditions. Your first-hand experience in the Army gave her more time. I think you should return to medical school."

He turned his head to hide his scowl. *You sound like my mother and my sisters,* he groused.

"Did I say something wrong?" Rhonda asked after a mile of silence.

"I'm doing what I want to do."

"Roger, as an ER doc, I save lives almost every day. You could do the same."

He snorted as he recalled patching up wounded soldiers with enemy bullets flying around him. "Been there, done that," he said flatly.

She nodded. "I know, but—"

He cut her off. "No more talk."

SIX HOURS LATER, Rhonda turned off the gravel road and plowed through a foot of snow up a long gravel driveway. She came to a stop and said, "We're here."

He took in the main house, a white, spacious two-story, wood-sided home. Behind the house were fenced pastures, a horse corral, a well-built cabin of the same design, a cavernous barn of weathered, unpainted wood next to a pitch-roofed, open-sided shed to shield a tractor, a flatbed truck, and an old Army jeep from the elements.

The dry, biting cold pierced his nostrils when he stepped out of the Suburban. He began to feel at home the second Rhonda led him up three wooden steps to the back porch. He followed her lead in removing his ice-caked boots before entering the kitchen door.

Hearty stew simmered in two black iron kettles on a commercial size white enamel stove. After six hours on the road, the tantalizing aroma of tender beef in the pot made his mouth water. The smell of bread in the oven came to him next. He looked up. From the ceiling, between the stove and the deep sink hung a wrought iron rack with hooks. From the hooks hung copper-plated pans with tin-coated cooking surfaces of every size.

A classic-looking Nordic woman, almost six feet tall, still lean, ruddy-cheeked, blonde hair streaked with silver, beautiful in her late fifties or early sixties, hugged Rhonda briefly, then gave Hitchcock a warm handshake. "We meet you at last, Roger! I'm Ingrid, Rhonda's mom. Rhonda talks about you constantly."

Rhonda is the mirror image of her mother. If she looks this good in her later years, he mused as he shook hands with Ingrid.

Minutes later a rough-hewn version of Hitchcock's

father removed his snow-caked boots on the porch and walked through the kitchen door in thick woolen socks. His grip, like his smile when they shook hands, was warm and strong. Hitchcock felt an immediate kinship with him.

"Pleased to meet you, Roger. I'm Einar, Rhonda's dad. The way our girl talks about you, I was beginning to wonder if you really existed or if Rhonda made you up!"

"Rhonda talks a lot about you to me too."

Einar grinned. "Let's bring your stuff in."

Jamie jumped out the second Hitchcock opened the back of the Suburban, woofing and wagging his tail at the sight of Einar. He leaned into Einar's rough rubbing of his head and neck, savoring the ritual of renewed friendship.

"Ah! Jamie, my nephew Karl's dog! Rhonda said she gave him to you. He was born right here on this ranch. How's he working out for you?"

"He's my constant companion when I'm not working, and my security man when I'm away."

"Looks like you keep him well fed and in top shape!" Einar exclaimed, beaming as he ran his hands over Jamie's shoulders and neck, checking his condition. "I'll take him to our sheltered kennel. We keep four Border Collies to help with the livestock and a Blue Tick hound for hunting and trailing. They won't fight. They grew up with each other."

Einar helped Hitchcock lug his bags upstairs. Like the rest of the house, the bedroom was clean, spacious and high-ceilinged, with a large window, gleaming hardwood floor, a four-post double bed, matching nightstand and dresser.

"This was our son Ed's room. The one we lost in Vietnam. We use it as a guest room now."

Einar set Hitchcock's bags on the bed and turned to him. "We're a Christian family, Roger. What you and our daughter do in Seattle is your business, but under our roof, only married couples sleep together."

"That's all right by me," he said, pleasantly surprised. "I came prepared to help with your work outside. I brought work clothes, boots and gloves."

"We can always use the help," Einar said, "but let's wash up first. Lunch is about ready. Then I'll show you around."

FIVE PLACE SETTINGS waited on a long oil-finished farm-style table, the top made of eight-inch-wide planks, two inches thick, topped with a steaming cast iron pot of vegetable beef stew, a platter of fresh dark brown bread, and a pitcher of milk.

A weathered, wiry Indian in his late forties removed his boots and acknowledged Hitchcock with a nod as he stepped inside.

"Billy, this is Roger, Rhonda's friend from the Coast," Einar said. They shook hands as Einar explained, "Billy's of the Nez Perce tribe. He's been with us over ten years now, so he's family. Our other hand is Sam. He's of the Sioux tribe, visiting his family in Montana for the holidays."

Einar and Ingrid exchanged approving glances when Hitchcock seated Rhonda before taking his seat. "Everything in the stew is from the ranch, only the milk is store-bought," Ingrid explained.

"We always give thanks before we dig in," Einar said. Ingrid, Rhonda and Billy bowed their heads as Einar folded his hands together. "Lord Jesus, we thank You for Your bounty, and for our guest. Please bless this food unto our bodies. In Your Name, amen."

As Hitchcock filled his bowl, Ingrid remarked, "You look Scandinavian, Roger, but both of your names are English."

"My dad was half English, half Norwegian, and my mother is full-blood Norwegian, but born here."

"Ah, from the look of you I didn't think you'd be Swedish. Do you speak any Norsk?" Ingrid asked. "That's what we are too, both sides from Norway."

"Not a word, I'm afraid."

A brief silence ensued as they took to eating. Hitchcock's first taste delighted him. The chunks of beef melted in his mouth, the carrots, peas cauliflower and potatoes were tender and needed no salt. "This is the finest stew I've ever tasted, Mrs. Kringen," he said.

"Thank you, Roger, and call me Ingrid," she replied

happily.

Rhonda winked at him as he tasted a buttered slice of warm bread. Its hearty flavor reminded him of the breads he read and heard about in Sunday school Bible stories. He smiled at the first bite. "This is really a rare treat for me."

He felt at home with Rhonda's family. The silence of Einar and Billy didn't bother him, for he understood they had been working outdoors in the cold all morning. Einar shared in the conversation with smiles and nods, while Billy focused on eating.

"You like the bread too?" Ingrid asked him, her face beaming. "I made it today."

"Don't I know it," he said, nodding his head. "I smelled it when I came through the kitchen. I was so sure I saw my name on it, that if Rhonda hadn't been watching me, I'd of snuck a piece, I was so hungry."

They all laughed together.

AN ICY WIND blew as Hitchcock followed Einar outside after lunch. He turned up the collar of his gray wool Filson coat as his eyes took in the barn, bunkhouse, sheltered livestock pens and corrals. "From here to Canada is a short drive as-the-crow-flies, and only twenty minutes to the Idaho state line," Einar explained.

"I see only horses. Any cattle?"

"We run over two hundred head on almost four hundred acres with leased grazing rights on the

National Forest adjacent to us."

"What breed?"

"We've settled on Red or Black Angus because the meat is not too fat, nor too lean."

Hitchcock pulled his leather gloves on. "We have a couple hours before dark, so put me to work."

Einar grinned. "As you wish!"

REPAIRING AND RESETTING a broken gate with Einar between the livestock pens in the cold invigorated Hitchcock. He felt new energy and satisfaction as his eyes took in the changing hues of the cloudless sky and fading sunset by the time they finished.

"Gets dark early, this time of year," Einar said. "Let's bring the horses into the barn and fed, then we're done."

Childhood memories of his family's horses came back as he helped Einar halter five horses and lead them into individual stalls in the barn. He savored the fragrance of fresh grain and Timothy hay as he portioned some to each horse and rubbed them down.

Rhonda was right: What he needed was fresh air, hard work, quiet, and home cooking. Just the first afternoon of outdoor physical work was head-clearing for him. The aroma of dinner on the stove sharpened his appetite as he removed his boots before coming into the kitchen with Einar and Billy.

Einar and Ingrid exchanged brief glances of

approval when Hitchcock again seated Rhonda next to him before seating himself.

"I see you brought a rifle," Einar commented as he forked into his second helping of roast beef.

"My late father's. A pre-'64 Winchester Model 70 in .270. Dad killed deer and elk with it, and a bear once, too."

".270? Excellent choice. A flat-shooting round for open country like this. It must have special meaning for you."

"It does," he answered softly.

"Can you shoot well with it?"

"My dad thought so."

"Bring it with you tomorrow morning."

"Sure. What are we doing?"

"Part of our herd is farther up near the tree-line where our land adjoins National Forest. The snow is thinner and they can graze on the exposed grass. We take our hay wagon up to feed them every morning."

"I suppose there are deer around, too, but I don't have a hunting license," Hitchcock said as he sliced himself another hunk of roast beef.

Einar shook his head. "Deer season is over. Coyotes and wolves are preying on calves and old ones in this cold 'cause they're easier pickings than deer or elk. If you can shoot, I'll need your help for predator control. You sure you don't mind?" Einar asked with a friendly wink.

"What time?"

"Breakfast at four. Can you make it?"

"Sounds like huntin' camp to me. I better hit the sack early."

As he finished laying out his clothes, rifle, ammunition and binoculars for the morning, he heard a soft knock at the door. Rhonda, in her nightgown and thick socks, rushed into his arms without a word, kissing him hungrily, her arms around his neck.

He held her tightly. "Shhh! You're not supposed to be in here! What if your dad sees you?"

She backed out of his room, blowing kisses. He laid on the bed, wide awake after her advances. Now he'd lose precious time trying to fall asleep.

BITING COLD AND the exertion of lifting and stacking hundred-pound bales of hay onto a flatbed truck awakened Hitchcock more than breakfast or coffee. He sat next to Billy as Einar drove slowly across ice-crusted snow-covered pasture, headlights pierced the low-lying clouds and darkness.

Dark shapes of cattle bunched together ambled toward them for their morning feed. Einar counted heads as Hitchcock opened the bales. As they moved on to the next group and repeated the procedure, Einar seemed worried.

"I'm missing three calves, two cows and a bull from this herd. It'll be daylight soon, then we'll hunt for them," he told Hitchcock.

"Wolves?"

Einar nodded. "They come down from Canada in packs during the winter. Coyotes are more plentiful but they're too small to take down big animals. They'll eat newborn calves as they are being born if there are enough of them. Under all that fur they're small and thin. Wolves can take down full-grown steers. What concerns me is I'm not seeing any carcasses."

"Maybe they drag their kills to a den to feed their young."

Einar shook his head. "Not the entire animal."

"Maybe the carcasses are under the snow."

"Haven't had new snow in days," Billy added.

SUNRISE DISPERSED THE darkness a half-hour later. The white blanket of snow magnified the sunlight a hundred times over. Einar wore sunglasses as he drove at idle speed while Hitchcock scanned ahead, binoculars raised to his eyes. He tapped Einar's shoulder.

"Coyote or young wolf on the ridge."

Einar stopped. Hitchcock studied the animal with his binoculars. "It's eating something, either unaware of us or ignoring us." He handed the binoculars to Einar.

"I'm seeing two, but only the head of the second one," Einar said. "Coyotes for sure. About two hundred yards."

"We're downwind," Hitchcock noted.

His boots crunched frozen snow as he slipped out of the cab, rifle in hand, careful to avoid making noise by shutting the door. He knelt, gently bolted a round into the chamber, flipped the safety off. He nestled the rifle against his shoulder, and put the crosshairs of the scope on the animal's shoulder. He inhaled, let the air halfway out, held the rest and squeezed the trigger. *Bang!* The coyote lifted a couple inches then flopped lifelessly to the ground. The other 'yote disappeared in a flash.

"Great shot!" Einar exclaimed in a low voice.

He grinned. *That one's for you, Dad.* "Thanks, Einar. Let's hike up there to check it out."

On the crest of the hill, they found the frozen carcass of a calf, disemboweled about a day earlier. The dead coyote lay next to it. Fifty yards away they spotted the rotting remains of another calf.

Einar cursed under his breath. "The calf carcasses don't account for the missing adults. Missing or dead cattle threatens our survival," he said. "The greater their numbers, the bolder coyotes become. Traps and poison work, but they also put good dogs at risk, so we don't use them."

"What's the solution?"

"What you did just now. 'Coyotes are survival experts. No one has been able to eradicate them. They are quick to adapt and repopulate. If you want to help us protect our livestock, you can spend your mornings out here with your rifle, shooting coyotes and wolves."

Hitchcock laughed heartily. "If this gets any better, I ain't goin' back!"

HE RODE WITH Einar and Billy in the Jeep the next morning through bitter cold to feed the cattle. They found the first herd bedded down in a swale, protected by a grove of pines on the opposite hill. He estimated the distance to the herd at two hundred yards, the pines another sixty. Einar glassed the area with binoculars as night yielded to morning.

"We've disturbed the environment by our arrival," Billy whispered. "Wait ten minutes for things to settle."

Hitchcock's eye caught movement. Three dark shapes of either wolves or coyotes crept slowly in a start-and-stop fashion from the tree line toward the unsuspecting bovines. They dropped to their bellies with each stop, their dark shapes contrasting with the snow.

Steam from his breath revealed they were downwind from the herd. Hitchcock unsheathed his rifle. They waited long minutes in the silent cold, neither moving nor speaking.

He remembered his father as he knelt and put the crosshairs of his scope on the leading one and flicked the safety off. The boom cracked the stillness and cattle milled about in frightened, mooing confusion. The two other predators bolted back to the protection of the trees, but the lead one lay stone-still.

"Let's give the cattle a few minutes to calm down before we check."

After waiting, Hitchcock and Einar trudged through the snow to the top of the ridge.

"Just as I feared—a wolf, the last thing we want around here. Still, that's two down this morning," Einar remarked as he stared at the large steel-gray carcass. "The two that got away are close by. They'll try again. We'd best move the herds closer to the ranch, today."

Hitchcock glassed the tree-line with his binoculars. "You're right. They won't leave a ready food supply in this cold. They're above us in the trees, waiting for us to leave so they can return to their meal."

"If you can kill another one, don't hesitate," Einar said.

"Not seeing any now, but..."

"Let's combine the herds and move them closer to the ranch while it's daylight."

As the sky grew lighter, they jolted across open terrain in the jeep, checking on the other two herds. When they paused to count the second herd, Hitchcock noticed that Einar again seemed troubled.

"I'm missing two more heifers from this herd since yesterday," he said. "We've got to move the herds down to the ranch—fast! Then we'll get our rifles and kill as many wolves today as we can."

"I see a couple strays grazing up in the tree-line," Hitchcock said.

"Horses work best to round up cattle in snowy conditions. We'll get Billy and Rhonda and the collies to help. Hope you can ride as well as you shoot!"

"I grew up riding," Hitchcock said, a happy grin spreading across his face.

CHAPTER EIGHTEEN
Rustlers

AN HOUR LATER Hitchcock rode behind Einar, Rhonda and Billy on horseback, trotting uphill across thin snow crust, the four Border Collies sniffing the air as they raced ahead. At Einar's direction they took a shortcut through a stand of pines in order to approach the farthest herd. They heard the sounds of men shouting, a truck engine sputtering and hooves upon metal.

They came to the edge of a clearing and spotted six cattle fifty yards away in a portable corral, being driven into a stock trailer by two men waving their arms.

"They're stealing our cattle!" Einar shouted. They trotted as fast as they dared across the snow-covered meadow.

The two thieves spotted them, slammed the trailer

shut and scrambled into the truck, leaving the portable corral and one calf behind. Tires spun in the snow, unable to gain traction.

"Get this thing moving!" He heard one of the men shout. The four tires whirred and spun, digging ruts in the snow. The driver goosed the gas repeatedly, creating a rocking motion until the truck began inching forward. Hitchcock was closing in when he saw the passenger roll the window down and aim a revolver into the air.

A shot was fired. Hitchcock opened his coat and gripped the revolver holstered on his belt. He knew the shot was a warning to come no closer. The surrounding wall of upward sloping ground, dense stands of timber and the absolute stillness intensified the blast. Einar raised his arm, but the riders, horses and dogs had already been stunned into a halt.

The rustlers were twenty yards away on the uphill side of a swale. Hitchcock grabbed his binoculars and dismounted. "Everybody remember the plate number I call out," he shouted.

Billy took out the pen and pocket-size notepad he used to record livestock conditions. "Trailer plate number Adam Seven Five Nine Eight Tom! The truck—can't see the plate, the trailer's in the way. White Ford one-ton with dual wheels!"

The truck gradually gained enough traction to begin pulling away.

"Got it. Trailer A7598T. White Ford one-ton with

duallies," Billy repeated while the others watched the truck and trailer amble across the snowy meadow to a former logging road in the distant tree line.

"Time is critical. Gotta get to a phone to run the trailer plate for the owner's name."

"Go! We'll move the herds together. Meet you at the house," Einar replied.

He backtracked to the house, keeping his horse to a trot. Twice it slipped in the snow but didn't fall. From the house he placed a long-distance call to Records. He had the results by the time the others returned.

"The trailer belongs to a Tom Caldwell on Hopkins Road. Do you know him?"

"What a shame this is," Einar said, sadness in his voice. "For years I did business with Tom. His sons own the place since he died. They're both ex-cons. The oldest boy just got out of Walla Walla."

"We've no time to lose, Einar," Hitchcock said.

"What do you have in mind?" Einar asked.

"Take me to the Caldwell place."

A FIVE-MILE DRIVE along a two-lane gravel road ended at a ranch where the house, barn and outbuildings were visible from the road. Hitchcock saw the mailbox at the beginning of the driveway read CALDWELL on the side.

From the side of the road, Hitchcock, Einar and Billy spotted at least two dozen cattle inside a holding pen and a white pickup and stock trailer in the back. "Looks like the same rig," Billy remarked.

Focusing his binoculars, Hitchcock said, "The plate on the trailer is A7598T, Washington, same as this morning. The truck looks to be the same, but I still can't see the plate because the trailer is in the way. Now we go to the sheriff's office."

AT THE PEND Oreille County Sheriff's Office in Newport, Hitchcock flashed his badge and police ID card to the desk clerk. She ushered him, Einar, and Billy into the detective office. They filed a complaint in the form of signed statements. Detective Norquist's double chin quivered slightly as he nodded with recognition as he read the statements.

"Umm-hmm. The Caldwell boys, Oliver and Earl. Nothing but trouble, those two. In and out of jail constantly, more in than out. Both did hard time at Walla Walla. Earl just got paroled last summer. Their old man, Tom, died last year from cancer. His ole lady, Jolene, died a dozen years ago—heart attack. Times must be hard if the boys'r stooping to stealing cattle."

Norquist shoved a pencil and a blank sheet of paper in front of Einar. "Draw me a sketch of your brand, Einar, then date and sign it. I'll write the affidavit, then we'll see the judge for a search warrant. After that, wait at home for a call from us."

BY THE TIME the day was almost gone, the phone at the Kringen Ranch rang. "Bring yer stock trailer to the Caldwell place, Einar. We got nine cattle here with yore brand," Detective Norquist said.

Hitchcock watched as Einar and Billy hitched the stock trailer to the one-ton Ford pickup, loaded the four Border Collies into the back. They headed for the Caldwell ranch.

IT WAS DARK and the temperature had dropped when Einar, Billy and Hitchcock met Detective Norquist and a deputy at the Caldwell place. They saw Ollie and Earl in the back of a patrol car, on their way to jail. Five steers, three calves and a bull were penned inside a small corral. Einar and Billy inspected them briefly. "They have my brand, all right," Einar confirmed.

The cattle were jittery from yelling, being moved, and the gunfire. They clambered into the trailer, then bolted back out in a panic, the adults mooing and grunting, the calves bawling. The ground, slippery with mud, snow and ice, made for dangerous footing when the only light came from headlights and flashlights and the smallest animal easily weighed five hundred pounds.

"Nuts to this. One of us'll slip and be trampled at this rate," Einar said as he recovered from slipping. "Stand back, Roger. Billy, let the dogs out."

"Nate, Jake, Gus, Beau, Round 'em up!" Einar

141

shouted with a wave of his arms. The four Border Collies, black and white dogs weighing between forty and fifty pounds of steel-hard muscle, plunged with joy and zeal into their work.

Hitchcock watched with amazement as Einar and Billy directed the dogs with blunt commands, then stepped back to watch them do what they were born to do. They barked and rushed at the steers and calves, herding them until they had nowhere to go but into the stock trailer. Billy slammed the gate shut when the last steer got in.

"Amazing!" Hitchcock exclaimed, grinning ear-to-ear. "Did you train them?"

Einar smiled as his dogs hopped back into the truck with only a hand signal. "Barely. Border Collies are so smart and bred for working with livestock, they pretty much figure out what you want done and train themselves."

RHONDA AND HER mother had gone to bed by the time they released the recovered cattle into a fenced pen. The men removed their mud-caked boots on the wooden porch, fed and bedded the dogs in the mud room and walked softly inside.

"Let the women sleep. This calls for a toast," Einar said in a low voice as he produced a bottle of cognac and three glasses.

A glowing, crackling fire, cognac and man-talk

made for a fit finish to a rare adventure which they relived and embellished as they drank, then the talk turned to the war, the political climate, boxing, and police work, until the embers died and the cognac too.

CHAPTER NINETEEN
Saturday Night at the Dew Drop Inn

DURING THE FIRST two hours of daylight, Hitchcock and Billy cruised the fences in the open-sided Jeep, making repairs where needed as they worked, hands and feet numbed from the cold. Resetting fence poles in earth frozen as hard as concrete refreshed him. He felt his mind and body mending and recharging as he labored, sweating under his clothes.

Movement in the tree line across the meadow caught Hitchcock's eye. He searched the undergrowth with his rifle scope. There being no wind to cause movement in the brush, he kept looking until he spotted the outline of a wolf. It was upwind, inching on its belly toward the herd through tall clumps of dead grass. Hitchcock laid prone in the snow, using his coat as a rifle rest, for the shot would be over four hundred yards.

Billy flashed a smile of approval as he kept digging. More details of the gunfight came to mind as he peered into his rifle scope. In his mind's eye he saw the rear window of the Ford Maverick, blazing gunfire in the dark, flying chunks of glass. A blonde woman in the driver seat, turning, aiming at him, he saw and heard the muzzle flash of her gun.

Movement in his scope brought him back to the present. He focused on the outline of a wolf. It spasmed at the shot and laid still.

DURING LUNCHTIME, EINAR glanced around the table. "No more work this afternoon. We rest, then clean up. The four of us are going to town tonight."

"I didn't bring dress clothes. Didn't expect to go out."

Einar grinned patiently. "Out here, Roger, dress clothes for Saturday night are clean jeans and shirt, manure brushed off your boots, and your hair slicked down."

WHAT A PLACE The Dew Drop Inn was. A classic roadhouse diner, white-washed wood siding, a low-pitch red asphalt shingle roof, scarred, two-inch thick wooden door with black nail heads in its stained deep brown surface.

Inside, a raised stage in the corner, white-washed wood walls, a clean-smelling fresh pine sawdust floor, bare light bulbs strung along the ceiling, long wooden picnic tables covered with red and white checkerboard tablecloths held grilled ribs and fried chicken, mashed potatoes and gravy, cold beer, women in dresses, and men in jeans and wool shirts.

A band of three men and a woman from Kentucky, all in their twenties, had been held over for a second week by popular demand, captivating the locals with authentic old-time Bluegrass music—banjo, fiddle, guitar and dulcimer.

Never had Hitchcock heard musicianship like this. He danced with Rhonda to fast-paced instrumentals like *Rabbit Up A Gum Stump, Hell Broke Loose in Georgia,* and *Pumpkin Rock.* An excited cheer went up and the benches emptied out to the dance floor when the guitar player struck the first notes of what had become everyone's favorite, *My Dixie Darlin',* sung by the girl.

The romantic rusticity of ranch life and now this revived his inner man. After the losses of his father, then Ruby, and being spit on when he came home from the war, he felt free from the past. He joined Rhonda and the rest of the crowd when they clapped and men's heavy boots thundered on the floor as they danced and cheered at the end of *My Dixie Darlin'* and the crowd shouted "More!" "More!" "Play it again!"

And the band obliged.

He took Rhonda in his arms and whirled her to the lyrics a second time.

"Would you look at those two, Ingrid! Roger's quite the dancer!" Einar exclaimed. Ingrid squeezed her husband's hand mightily and her eyes watered up as she watched her daughter and Hitchcock together. Ingrid began sobbing as Einar slipped his arm around her shoulders, "I know, I know," he said softly.

The road back was dark and icy. Einar stopped to engage the four-wheel-drive unit by turning the locking front hubs.

"Church tomorrow. We leave at eight for the nine o'clock service," Ingrid said.

Hitchcock said nothing. He didn't know how to tell Einar and Ingrid he hadn't been a church-goer since he joined the army.

CHAPTER TWENTY
Whisperings Down the Hall

EINAR LAID IN bed next to Ingrid, knowing what her muffled sobbing was about. He gently took her hand in his and waited.

"You see what I see, don't you?" she asked.

"Yeah," he said in a soft whisper. "Roger is so much like Ed in the way he moves, thinks and reasons I can hardly believe it. He's passionate and deliberate like Ed was. He even handles chores and rides like Ed did."

He turned his head to Ingrid. "What do you think will happen? He's quite a bit younger than Rhonda."

Einar couldn't see his wife's smile in the dark as she tapped his arm. "So? Aren't you about that many years younger than me, or did you forget, *young man*?"

He laughed a quiet belly laugh. "How could I *ever* forget your folks and mine calling you cradle-robber!"

Ingrid paused for a few seconds. "I think," she said, analyzing, "Roger's not ready yet, but Rhonda's mind is made up. She's never been like this about anyone. I predict she'll pursue Roger until he catches her."

If Ingrid could have seen her husband's face, she'd see him smiling. The smile was in his voice too as he said, "Yep, that's our girl."

† † †

THE HOUSE WAS quiet and dark. The half-moon shone its cold light brightly on the frozen snow, creating a ghostly, other-world setting outside. Alone in the gloom, lying supine in bed, Hitchcock stared at the barely visible ceiling, listening to a nearby pack of coyotes howling and yipping over a fresh kill, calling the pack to come in for the feast. The ruckus became hungry growls of carnivores tearing into warm blood and meat.

But Hitchcock's mind was elsewhere.

Tonight, he found it strange that he should find peace at last over the losses of his father and Ruby just by going to a country dance. How could it happen? No longer were they issues he couldn't get past. They were *chapters* in his life now. His father's influence would guide him for the rest of his days, and Ruby was a lesson he wouldn't go through again. His time at the ranch somehow freed him of looking back to earlier, happier times, toying with useless thoughts of what-if and if-only-this-or-that happened.

With freedom from the past came clearer details of the gunfight. His mind was settled at last for whatever outcome the inquest had in store.

CHAPTER TWENTY-ONE
Sunday Surprise

TO HITCHCOCK'S DISMAY, the church service lacked the religious chill of his childhood experience. The small congregation was genuine, warm and welcoming. The pastor surprised him the most. Instead of the stagnant piety he saw in pastors, priests, and church-goers, he found this fiery young preacher, no older than himself, a refreshing change. Ruggedly-built, an outdoor sort, a logger and a smoke jumper before and after his Christian conversion, he preached powerfully about the requirement of true repentance as essential to conversion and must be ongoing to live the Christian life. His words resonated with Hitchcock.

"Being a church-goer, or even a church worker won't cut it, folks. At the end of your days, when you stand before the lord, if that's all you've done, the Lord will say 'Away from Me. I never knew you," he said. His words grabbed Hitchcock's attention.

"Just as walking in and out of a garage will never make you a car, going in and out of church won't make you a Christian. To enter heaven when your days are over, you must repent of your sins to become a Christian and enter heaven at the end of your life."

Hitchcock leaned forward, focusing on every word the pastor said. "What must one do to meet that requirement? you ask. The answer in one word: repent. It's all through the bible. If you haven't confessed your sins to God through Christ, and *deliberately* turned away from them in your heart, you are *not* saved. You're not Christian."

How come I never heard this in the church I grew up in? Hitchcock wondered. The pastor's words caused stirring among the small congregation. Hitchcock focused on what the pastor would say next.

"This is a hard teaching, but the fact is, your name isn't written in the Lamb's Book of Life if you haven't repented," the pastor said matter-of-factly. "At the end of your days, you won't go to heaven, no matter how much good you did for God or in God's Name. Now – God knows we will still sin after we're saved, so we must repent and ask forgiveness as soon as we become aware of it. God forgives us in a split-second, so we don't need to grovel. No, God wants His people to be bold, to hold our heads high, for as Christians, our lives are endless. When we have the Holy Spirit in us, we are part of the Holy Trinity. To win others to Christ when they see our changed behavior is the job of each of us after we receive salvation. God wants each of us to be a living letter of hope and salvation from Him to the unsaved."

HE WAITED IN line to shake the preacher's hand at the door after the service. "I'm Roger, a visitor here," he began.

The preacher smiled. They shook hands. "I wish everybody was as attentive to the sermon as you were," he said.

"I'll be here a few more days," Hitchcock said, "could we meet for a talk? I'm staying with the Kringen family."

"You bet. I have Tuesday open. Say ten o'clock, here?"

"Sounds good. See you then."

"WHY DID YOU want to see the pastor before we leave?" Rhonda asked on the way back to the ranch.

"He's got something I want," he said at last.

"What?"

"I don't know," he replied, shrugging. "But whatever it is, it's good, and I want it."

EARLY THE NEXT morning, as Hitchcock rode out with Billy driving the jeep to feed the cattle and further reduce the coyote population if possible, more details of the gunfight came into focus.

A PHONE CALL from Captain Holland came in at the ranch at lunchtime, ordering Hitchcock and Sherman to appear before a Medical Examiner's Inquest on Thursday. The following morning, he and Rhonda said their goodbyes to everyone and began the long drive back, Hitchcock wondering what fate awaited him on the other side.

CHAPTER TWENTY-TWO
Ocean Shores

DAMP COLD AND a raw, driving wind numbed Sherman's face and hands as he dug for clams on the wind-swept beach of the Washington coast. He smiled at the reddened cheeks and running noses of his son and daughter, five and four, respectively. "Tide's coming in and we've all had enough cold and wind," he said, picking up the buckets and clam shovels.

Karen heated up leftover oyster stew from the day before, with fresh bread and hot cocoa for the kids, while he built a crackling driftwood fire in the stone fireplace. The hot meal and the switch from cold to warm quickly drained the kids of their energy. They snuggled with their mom and dad on a bearskin rug in front of the fire.

Moments after Sherman started reading them a bedtime story, Karen saw they had fallen asleep. He covered them with a blanket and sat with Karen on the couch, watching the fire, in a mood of reflective silence.

"Can I bring you anything? Coffee, a glass of wine?"

He shook his head and drew her close to him, holding his silence, mesmerized by the fire. He didn't think he'd need time off after the shooting because the Army never gave time off after firefights, but now he was glad to have it. They took the kids out of school, taking along Bud, the family Golden Retriever, and kicked back at his parents' beach cabin at Ocean Shores.

Sensing that Tom would open up, Karen laid in his arms on the couch, waiting.

"While you slept last night, details of the shooting began coming back," he said at last, still staring at the fire, "more came into focus today while we were on the beach."

"Tell me what happened. I want to know."

Sherman paused before he said, "We almost made a fatal mistake by walking up to a rolling stolen after it crashed without our guns drawn. We dropped our guard, I guess, because we saw two women in the front seat. They weren't moving, so we figured they were hurt. I remember thinking the women were lucky to have Roger there because he was a medic in 'Nam."

"Sounds logical," Karen said in support.

"Not really. We were naïve and careless, considering the situation and our experience level."

"How so?" she asked.

"The guy hiding on the back floor was waiting for us, shotgun in hand. We didn't see him until he opened fire."

Karen gasped, but said nothing.

"When a stolen car crashed when it tried to outrun us. We should have had our guns drawn as we approached, even though injuries from the crash were likely. Because we saw only women and thought they had to be hurt, our guard was down. I was shocked when the rear window suddenly exploded and here was this guy aiming a shotgun at us, ready to shoot again. We were caught off guard, big time."

"Ah!" she said, expressing surprise and understanding.

"We were without excuse," Sherman said, gazing into the fire, "We knew about the car being stolen and the murdered girl it belonged to. So, there we were, completely surprised by this guy on the back floor trying to kill us. Roger drew his gun and started shooting to stop him before he could fire again. The woman in the driver seat turned around and aimed a pistol at Roger. Without thinking I started shooting to stop her from shooting Roger."

"Didn't you shoot the guy with the shotgun?"

He shook his head. "As I remember it now, Roger was so fast he had already shot him several times in the head before I drew and fired once. With Guyon dead, my instinct was to shoot the driver to save Roger. I was in such a hurry that I didn't aim, I just emptied my gun at her through the driver seat. She dropped her gun and slumped forward. The shotgun went off a second time, only because Guyon's finger was on the trigger. His second shot went wild."

Karen remained in her husband's arms in stunned silence. "Wow, honey," she finally said. "Is there any more?"

"Yes, but not yet. As I experienced in the Army, recall comes in pieces."

"Sounds like Roger saved your life by killing the guy with the shotgun, and you saved his by shooting the driver." She slipped her arm around his neck. "I'm proud of you, Tom. I was so fearful when I heard about the gunfight—there aren't words for the relief I felt when I knew you came through unhurt."

She curled into almost a fetal position in his lap. "I live in constant fear that one of these times you won't make it back to me," she said, sobbing softly.

He held her close, absorbing her warmth. After almost six years of happy marriage, he knew her thoughts, that she wanted him to leave police work, but respected him too much to say it. He also knew Karen understood he would never leave law enforcement.

"Let's leave early enough to take a round trip train ride from Mukilteo to Wenatchee so the kids can see the snow in Stevens Pass before I report back on Thursday."

She started to fall asleep in Sherman's arms. "Sure, hon," she whispered.

TWO DAYS LATER, like a fog which finally lifted, more details of the shooting came back to Sherman as the train chugged through the snow-clad, rocky canyons and trickling waterfalls of Stevens Pass. He said nothing to Karen. What he remembered disturbed him.

CHAPTER TWENTY-THREE
The Inquest

THE TENSE DRIVE to the King County Courthouse in Seattle ended with an exasperating hunt for a parking space. Despite the cool, cloudy morning, the white dress shirt under Hitchcock's suit was drenched with nervous sweat by the time he found a space on the steep slope of the County parking lot on 5th Avenue and James Street. His stomach churned as he checked his Timex and walked two blocks downhill to the courthouse. He rode a packed elevator to the fourth floor in silence.

He found Sherman sitting on a bench outside the courtroom. "We're to wait here until they call us," he said.

He made no reply as he sat next to Sherman. Neither of them knew what to expect as they squirmed on the bench. Hitchcock felt like an insect waiting to be placed under a microscope. The clicking sounds of footsteps as people passed them on the marble floor, clinical and impersonal, added to his anxiety.

He knew that he and Sherman were in the right, but would the inquest panel agree? They had no qualms about killing; they had killed before in combat, but with society's changing attitudes toward veterans and cops, would their war experience be used against them?

The killing they did as soldiers in combat, and now as cops, essentially soldiers of the civilian courts, was under lawful authority, yet, due to the attitudes of the Brass and the city manager's crowd, Hitchcock knew no rest. Who could he and Sherman trust? Despite their supervisors' assurances of fair treatment, they felt the accusing heat of being on trial.

Of the two, Hitchcock had more reason to be nervous: Reporter Steve Miller warned him that there were secret plans within the Department to fire him and Sherman. He hadn't yet mentioned it to Sherman. What good would it do? And what would Sherman think of his being on friendly terms with a reporter?

Before the inquest even started, the shooting changed the Department. Besides the one or two times an officer shot at a fleeing felon and missed, or dispatched a suffering dog or horse, officer-involved shootings were beyond the Department's experience.

Seattle PD, the largest police agency in the state, relied on the coroner's inquest to decide if an officer-involved shooting was justified. The procedure kept internal politics out of decision making.

"When a shooting in King County results in the death of a person, the County Coroner decided whether or not to have an inquest," Sergeant Breen explained to Hitchcock and Sherman the day before the hearing. "An inquest is similar to a trial in which six citizens review the facts, only to decide if the shooting was justified."

"Aren't we afforded legal counsel?" Hitchcock asked.

"Nope," Breen replied.

Incredulous, Hitchcock asked, "Why?"

"Because you're not on trial, Roger. The inquest panel's only function is to determine if the shooting was justified."

"And if the panel decides the shooting wasn't justified?"

"It still doesn't necessarily mean the officers will be charged. The county prosecutor decides whether or not to file criminal charges, based on other influencing factors."

"That sucks, Sarge, and you know it," Hitchcock snapped.

Before Sergeant Breen could respond, Sherman asked, "What happens if the panel rules the shooting was justified?"

Sergeant Breen shrugged. "The officers are exonerated by the judge and automatically return to duty, naturally."

Hitchcock and Sherman exchanged nervous

glances. Neither said a word.

ACROSS LAKE WASHINGTON, every member of the Department waited to see what would happen to Hitchcock and Sherman for pulling their triggers on two armed felons until their guns were empty. Not a few rank-and-file officers assumed both would be fired, even prosecuted, abandoned by the Brass.

The clandestine "third floor faction" of City Hall licked its collective chops, intending to exploit the shooting, no matter how justified, to advance their agenda. Lieutenant Bostwick politicked among the Department Brass for an internal investigation of both officers, over which he would preside.

But thanks to Captain Delstra's own mouse in the corner, he was a step or two ahead of Bostwick. He knew every step and every detail of Bostwick's plot. Delstra, the former Marine, realized the irreparable damage that would befall the Department if the first two officers in the agency's history to be involved in a shooting were maligned for purely political reasons.

To protect Hitchcock and Sherman from the ill will of the third floor and collaborative elements within the Department, Delstra convinced Chief Carter to follow Seattle's example by letting the matter be examined and decided at the county level.

Judge Charles V. Wickham was presiding. A deputy prosecutor would present evidence and call witnesses to testify. Six citizens were chosen from the jury rolls to be on the deciding panel. The rules authorized the judge to overrule the panel's decision if he felt they failed to follow the rules in reaching their decision.

Hitchcock and Sherman waited on the bench, fidgeting, saying nothing as their peers and others filed past them into the courtroom. Hitchcock's anxiety increased when Captains Delstra and Holland passed them without acknowledging either of them.

CHAPTER TWENTY-FOUR
Testimony Begins

SERGEANT BREEN WAS first up. He testified that he arrived at the scene in time to witness the entire shooting. He saw the rear window of the Maverick burst into fragments, showering the officers with glass. He saw Hitchcock draw and began firing his weapon first, followed by Sherman. He then saw the driver turn and fire one shot from a handgun at Hitchcock. The shooting was still going on when she slumped forward, apparently as a result of being shot.

Detective Meyn testified regarding his recoded interview of Linda Ogilvie, which he played for the board members.

A stern-faced bailiff stepped into the hallway, made eye contact with Hitchcock and beckoned him with his forefinger.

Hitchcock felt sweat roll down his chest and his heart race as he entered the courtroom, packed with news reporters, administrators from his Department, and several black observers who scowled intensely at him.

Under questioning by the deputy prosecutor, he testified regarding the stolen car report he took at the scene of a drug overdose case in which Guyon was named as the suspect in the death of the owner of the car and its theft, that while on patrol with Sherman a few weeks later, he recognized the car as it crossed the freeway overpass. He testified that he feared for his life and returned fire when Guyon fired at him and Sherman from hiding in the back. He kept firing in an effort to stop Guyon from firing again.

Sherman testified regarding the pursuit of the stolen car, the two women in the front seat who appeared to be fighting just before the car swerved off the road into a telephone pole, that he didn't see Guyon on the rear floor until after the first shot blew out the rear window. He saw Hitchcock shooting Guyon, and he shot the driver until his gun was empty when she turned and aimed her gun at Hitchcock.

Dr. Banker testified regarding his findings of the autopsies he performed on Guyon and Driscoll. His testimony was followed by the state crime lab ballistics expert.

Detective Joe Small testified regarding the investigation of the shooting. "We reconstructed the shooting with careful comparison of the eyewitness testimonies of Sergeant Breen and Linda Ogilvie with those of the involved officers. We found no disparities. The decedent Guyon ambushed the officers by firing a double-barrel shotgun at them from a hiding position on the floor between the back and front seats of the vehicle as they approached to check the occupants in the front seat for injuries. The first blast blew out most of the rear window. We found that the officers responded in keeping with their training by returning fire in an effort to stop the decedent from firing again.

"The officers' holsters are in evidence because they prove the urgency of the moment when they drew their weapons right through the leather retention straps without unsnapping them. We preserved the Ford Maverick in an indoor, secure environment to process it as evidence and reconstruct the shooting. Between what we found in the car and what the autopsies revealed, we determined the officers fired a combined total of twelve rounds during the gunfire exchange. The decedent Guyon fired his shotgun a second time, but it discharged into the right rear panel of the car, below the window, not up at the officers. We conclude the decedent was dead when the second discharge of the shotgun went off because his finger was still on the trigger when Officer Hitchcock shot him. The decedent's convulsing caused the second barrel to discharge."

"Detective Small, what are your findings regarding the death of the driver, Mae Driscoll?" the deputy prosecutor asked.

"We found that as Officer Hitchcock fired his weapon at decedent Guyon, the driver, decedent Driscoll tried to fire her gun at Officer Hitchcock. Officer Sherman shot Driscoll shot twice through the back of the driver seat. One shot paralyzed her instantly, causing her to release her weapon, a .380 caliber automatic. Driscoll's shot missed Officer Hitchcock and struck the right rear corner of the roof of the car. The other shot, also fired by Officer Sherman, punctured Driscoll's aorta, which, according to the coroner's report I read, resulted in almost instant death from rapid blood loss."

"Thank you, Detective. Are there other findings?"

Detective Small held up a file folder. "I refer to State Crime Lab reports which have been admitted and testified to. Both bullets removed from the decedent Mae Driscoll were fired by Officer Sherman's weapon. The State Lab findings are consistent with our reconstructing the incident through examination of the vehicle, and interviews with both officers and their supervisor, Sergeant Breen, who witnessed the shooting.

"As has been previously testified by the witness for the State Crime Lab, their reports determined the two bullets recovered from the cranium of decedent Tyrone Guyon, and a third bullet recovered from the back of the front seat, were all fired from Officer Hitchcock's weapon."

"Is that all, Detective?" the prosecutor asked.

"Not quite. Five of the twelve rounds the officers fired struck the two decedents. We recovered the remaining seven bullets from the dashboard and the driver's seat."

"Can you give us an estimate of the total time involved in this exchange of gunfire?"

Two panel members shook their heads in dismay when Detective Small answered, "Based on eyewitness accounts, we estimate the entire shoot-out, which involved fifteen rounds fired by four combatants, lasted less than three seconds."

The prosecutor paused for a few seconds to let Detective Small's statement sink in. "You say fifteen rounds fired in three seconds, as in one-thousand-one, one-thousand-two, one-thousand-three, at a range of only nine to eleven feet, am I correct?"

"Correct," replied Detective Small.

A hushed silence fell over the courtroom. The deputy prosecutor addressed the bench. "Your Honor, as a representative of the Coroner's Office in this inquest, my presentation of the evidence rests."

Judge Wickham instructed the panel regarding its duties under the law. Everyone in the courtroom stood as the panel members adjourned to jury chambers to deliberate, followed by the Judge departing to his chambers.

"Let's grab a bite. The jury won't begin deliberations

until they've had lunch on the County dime. There are a lot of lunch spots close to the courthouse. Let's find a place, my treat" Breen told Hitchcock and Sherman.

THEY WALKED ACROSS Third Avenue from the courthouse to a hole-in-the-wall diner packed shoulder-to-shoulder with people dressed for court. Sherman barely touched the cup of soup he ordered. Hitchcock stuck with black coffee while Breen had a pastrami on rye. Only Breen talked, Hitchcock and Sherman were too nervous for conversation.

The jurors reconvened meeting after the noon break. After reviewing photographs of the scene and the evidence, reading lab and autopsy reports and officers' statements, and listening to the recorded dying declaration of Linda Ogilvie, the inquest panel notified the bailiff that they had reached their verdict.

Judge Wickham called the court to order. Hitchcock and Sherman stood with the rest of the courtroom as the inquest panel filed out of the jury chambers into the jury box and took their seats. Under his clothes, Hitchcock's skin quivered.

CHAPTER TWENTY-FIVE
The Verdicts

TWO HOURS LATER, the members of the inquest panel filed back into the courtroom. The blank expression on the weathered face of the foreman, a stout commercial fisherman, and the judge looking concerned as he watched the face of each panel member, caused Hitchcock to worry.

"Has the panel reached a verdict, Mr. Foreman?"

The fisherman got to his feet. "We have, Your Honor."

Hitchcock's heart pounded as the foreman handed a folded slip of paper to the bailiff, who handed it to the judge. A brief smile spread across Judge Wickham's face as he read the slip of paper.

"Has the panel followed the law and the rules of procedure in reaching this verdict?" the Judge asked.

"We have, Your Honor."

"Please state your findings to the Court."

The foreman nodded as he said, "After examining the evidence us, we find the officers were ambushed by armed criminals while performing their lawful duty in trying to stop a stolen car. When the decedents fired at them, they acted in defense of the community and themselves by returning fire. Both shootings were justified."

Judge Wickham nodded and smiled. "Very well, then. The officers are exonerated and may return to duty. Court is adjourned."

At the sound of the gavel, a rush of relief filled the courtroom followed by a round of relieved congratulations, back slapping and hand shaking.

When they reached the hallway, Sherman said to Hitchcock, "Let's meet for a schooner on our way home."

† † †

THE BARMAID AT the Midlakes Tavern left a pitcher of beer and two glasses on the table. Hitchcock was pensive as he watched Sherman fill both glasses.

"You saved my life, Tom."

"And you saved mine. Do you fully remember what you did?"

"Not everything. I remember a muzzle flash from the front seat," Hitchcock replied.

"I remembered more while we spent a few days at Ocean Shores," Sherman said. "The rest came back to me during a roundtrip train ride to Wenatchee with Karen and the kids."

"Tell me," Hitchcock said.

"I saw you pumping lead into Guyon's noggin before I drew my gun. He *had* to be dead. His shotgun was pointed at me, so you saved *my* life."

Sherman stopped, waiting for a response but Hitchcock said nothing.

"What I remember that wasn't in my testimony is that I saw you hesitate when Mae Driscoll pointed her gun at you," Sherman said. "You froze. I think it's because she was a woman. She was about to kill you, but instead of firing to protect yourself, you locked up. I emptied my gun as fast as I could to stop her."

Sherman paused, leaving Hitchcock stunned.

"This stays between us, Roger. We were in 'Nam. You know from being there that women can kill as readily as men. What if there's a next time? Will you or someone else be hurt or die because you hesitate to use force against a woman? Leave your chivalry at home when you come to work."

Hitchcock held his silence for long seconds. "I didn't remember it for quite a while," he finally said. "But I did see Driscoll turn in her seat and aim her gun at me. I had one bullet left. I can hardly believe I fired it at Guyon instead of her. Then I heard my gun clicking. Empty."

He paused to sip his beer, then went on. "I don't want to be a safety risk to anyone, Tom. Changing won't be easy. Hitting a woman, let alone shooting one goes against my upbringing, but I must change, and I will."

Sherman nodded and raised his glass. "A toast, then." They clinked their steins together and drank.

Hitchcock winced as he set his glass down.

"Something wrong?" Sherman asked.

"I have this feeling of alarm. Something is really wrong."

"I'm sure it'll clear up now."

Hitchcock ruefully shook his head. "It won't."

CHAPTER TWENTY-SIX
Outcomes

THE GUNFIGHT AND the exoneration of Hitchcock and Sherman had a celebratory effect on officers up and down the line. It had a maturing effect on the Department, and with it came higher credibility with the public.

Because the Brass supported Hitchcock and Sherman from the beginning, officers' long-held fear that the administration would sell out any officer who killed in the line of duty was laid to rest. The generational gulf between officers, including the administration, had been bridged.

A new *esprit de corps*, an air of unity, confidence and pride arose not only between the line officers and the Brass, but also between the Department and the public. The Department was viewed by the general public as capable of protecting them. For a time, at least, the often-acrimonious rift between some elements of the public and the men in blue mellowed out.

† † †

HIS PLANS THWARTED, Bostwick pouted as he and his anguished third-floor handlers watched, helpless, as Hitchcock and Sherman received commendation letters. The Brass directed them to share their experience with new officers in training and display their broken holster straps to show the effects of stress and adrenalin under fire. Neither of them knew it was Captain Delstra who protected them from the schemes of Bostwick and certain people on the third floor.

† † †

Shift Briefing

SERGEANT BREEN, GRINNING from the podium, announced "All right boys, we're glad Hitchcock and Sherman are with us again, and my, don't they look rested after an extra two-week vacation? The front desk is relieved that Hitchcock is back. Now the phone calls from single women asking, *"Is Roger coming back?"* Breen mimicked women callers in a squeaky voice "will finally stop!" Everyone laughed.

"A woman and her teenage son are upstairs asking for you. They came in while you were away. Don't know what they want," Breen told Hitchcock after briefing.

CHAPTER TWENTY-SEVEN
Triple Harvests

THE TALL, HUSKY teenage boy waiting in the lobby with his mother seemed familiar. "Officer Hitchcock? You probably don't remember me. Will Hodges. I gave you a lot of lip the night you arrested me at the Lake Hills Dance."

Hitchcock grinned sociably as he extended his hand. "Sure, I remember you, Will. How can I help?"

A sheepish grin came over Hodges. "I learned a lesson the night you put me in the cell with that huge old guy. He scared me so bad, I realized my life was on the wrong track. I told my mom what happened and how quickly you came to my rescue and treated me well—even after I treated you badly. I came to apologize, Officer Hitchcock.

"I can hardly believe the change in Will since you arrested him, Officer Hitchcock," Mrs. Hodges said.

"It's like the arrest flipped a switch in him. I waited, thinking he would go back to his old self in a couple weeks but he didn't. He does his chores around the house without being told, gets his homework done on time, his grades are better, and he works hard at the store. He reads all the news articles about you and the other officers. Hardly talks about anything else except becoming a police officer."

He looked at the lad, his face beaming.

"I work part-time at the Lake Hills Mayfair store now and my goal is to become a policeman when I reach my twenty-first birthday. I applied for the new cadet program a few minutes ago."

Hitchcock shook the lad's hand again. "Good on you, Will. You owned up to your mistakes like a man, you learned from them and moved on. You're a kid no more. Today you are one of us, a man, and you'll make a fine officer."

Hitchcock's words brought broad smiles to Will and his mother.

"I know who is selling drugs at my school. The main one is an older guy named Mike who hangs out in the parking lot after school, selling pot and other stuff," Will said.

"Mike? Long blond hair?" Hitchcock asked.

A look of surprise came over Will's face. "Uh, yeah. How did you know?"

Hitchcock turned to Will's mother. She looked

worried. "That man is dangerous, Will. We've been looking for him. If you see him on the school grounds again, call me but do nothing else, understand? *Nothing* else."

"What about the school authorities, Officer Hitchcock? As a parent, should I be the one to report this to them?" Will's mother fearfully asked.

"There's an element in the school faculty, Mrs. Hodges."

Shock swept over her face. "What?"

"You don't know who you can trust. You want your name and your son's name unmentioned—completely out of it." He searched their faces. "We have a new detective unit that specializes in cases involving juveniles. It's better for you if I get them involved without mentioning your names even to them. They'll handle it."

Mrs. Hodges appeared to relax. Hitchcock told her "If you're still comfortable with your son or yourself giving me information, of course I'll receive it. If I can't act on it myself, I'll pass it to the juvenile unit."

"I have names and information I can give you right now," Will said. Hitchcock handed him the notepad from his shirt pocket.

Will's mother spoke up. "Wait for me in the car, Will. Write down the names while I have a word with Officer Hitchcock. We'll give him the information before we leave."

Will went outside. Betty Hodges's eyes moistened as she squeezed Hitchcock's arm. "Drugs are destroying lives everywhere I turn," she said. "I didn't expect Will to offer to help you in this way. As long this doesn't put him in danger, he can report what he knows. God bless you, Officer Hitchcock. Will's dad abandoned us years ago. Hearing a man he admires give him recognition will encourage him to stay on the right path."

Will approached and handed the notepad back to Hitchcock. "These are five seniors who sell LSD and pot at school," he said.

Hitchcock scanned the list of names. He recognized three of them from previous arrests. "Thank you, both for coming to see me today. You've no idea how much it means to me to see a young life like Will's take a turn for the better. We'll stay in touch."

Will's mother wiped her eyes with a tissue as she said, "Thank you, officer, and keep up the wonderful work you are doing. Merry Christmas."

THAT MIKE SMITH, an adult, was able to enter the campus of Sammamish High School at will to sell drugs troubled Hitchcock. *How could it be that no one on the faculty noticed this or did anything? Patrol is looking for Smith, so how is it that he keeps slipping in and out of town unseen? Something is wrong.*

Radioing himself in service, having no calls holding, he took a different route to Eastgate; through Lake Hills, stopping at the neighborhood Chevron station where he saw Randy Fowler working on a customer's car.

"Hey, grease monkey, what time does this place close up?"

Randy leaned his face and grease-covered arms into the patrol car passenger window and smiled. "In a few minutes. How are ya? Been out of town, I hear."

"How did *you* know?" Hitchcock asked, incredulous.

Randy grinned and shrugged. "Heard it through the grapevine."

He shook his head in dismay, thinking, *Word travels fast in Eastgate!* "As long as I don't get a call in the next few minutes, I'll give you a lift home."

"Be ready in a minute."

They rode in silence until they reached Randy's house, then Randy opened up, "I'm glad Tyrone and Mae what's-her-name are dead, Roger. If you hadn't killed them, they'd never leave me or my family alone until they'd used up me and Connie till we was both dead, which would've killed Mom."

Hitchcock said nothing. Randy continued, "When I learned about the shooting on the news, I felt free at last to move forward with my life. By killing them, you saved my life a second time. I'm inspired to stay clean even more. I want to change. We held a family talk about Tyrone, the drug scene, and all that stuff. We agreed as a family to help you by telling you about other people like Tyrone. We hear things, so you'll be hearing from us but we don't want our names out. You gotta promise me."

"I promise."

Randy handed him a folded sheet of notepaper. "Here are two guys in my neighborhood who deal acid and cocaine out of their houses and at Robinswood Park, plus the names of the kids who buy from them and sell to others."

THE RADIO CRACKLED as he watched Randy enter his house. "Records to Three Zero Six, Switch to F2," he said into the mic.

"Urgent message for you to call Mata at the number you use."

He called her from a payphone. "Roger!" Gayle exclaimed. "About time you're back. Ronald Davis has taken over Tyrone Guyon's territory at The Hilltop, and Guyon's trailer in the park next door. He's there all the time now."

"What car is he using?"

"Same white Caddy. He has a new guy with him, the word is he's Davis's cousin. A huge guy, like a mountain, tall, about three hundred pounds, shaved head, very dark skin, goes by Leroy. A scary guy. Apparently, he's Davis's muscle and carries a gun."

"Where are they now?"

"At Guyon's trailer as of an hour ago. The word I

got tonight is that Davis has a new load of heroin with him. Also, he keeps a small gun hidden on him," she said.

"Where will you be later tonight?"

"Going home after closing at two, earlier if it's another slow night."

"I'll try to be there to help you close."

Hitchcock flipped through his notebook and keyed his radio mic "Three Zero Six, Records. Warrant check."

Dispatcher Patty replied: *"Go ahead, Three Zero Six."*

"Re-check for and confirm any warrants for Ronald Davis. DOB 7-8-45."

Four minutes later: *"Three Zero Six, King County confirms two outstanding felony warrants: a no-bail warrant for Armed Robbery for Ronald Watkins Davis. DOB 7-8-45. NMA, six feet two, one-eighty, brown and black. A second no-bail warrant is for Felon in Possession of a Firearm."*

He found Davis's Cadillac parked at the Eastgate Mobile Manor trailer park, unoccupied. The hood was cold. On F2 he radioed Sergeant Breen to meet him.

Minutes later Sergeant Breen pulled up next to Hitchcock outside the trailer park.

"What's up?"

"Got an armed felon in the trailer park named Ronald Davis with confirmed warrants for armed robbery and weapons charges," Hitchcock said. "According to my informant, Davis is in Tyrone Guyon's trailer but which trailer it is we don't know."

"Is this your Mata Hari again?"

"Yep. I got the same two felony hits on Davis's car a couple weeks ago at the Hilltop. I got called away before I could find him. The vehicle was gone when I returned. Mata says Davis has a huge new guy named Leroy with him as his enforcer. Both are packing heat."

"I'll ask the dicks which trailer belonged to Guyon," Breen said. "Next thing is the safety of the residents. We'll have to evacuate the place and call in Delstra's Tactical Arms Group. Meanwhile stay outside, at the exit, but out of sight. I'll get another unit here to help."

Breen keyed his mic: "Four Twenty to Three Zero Eight."

"Eight, go," Walker replied.

"Meet me immediately at the rear lot of Cascade Ford for a detail."

Hitchcock positioned himself at forty yards away at an angle where he could watch the entrance-exit of the trailer park. As far as he could see, no lights were on in any of the trailers. A light rain began falling, obscuring his view. He flipped the wiper switch. He estimated there were forty trailers in the park, all occupied. That meant at least eighty people would have to be evacuated before the TAG unit took action.

This would be the unit's first callout. Captain Delstra's creation. Like he did with the tactical squad, he put his career on the line when he bucked the Chief, the City Manager, and most of the City Council to create a special weapons team for situations like this. Hitchcock shook his head as he thought about evacuating almost a hundred people to arrest two dangerous men, armed felons with nothing to lose by resisting arrest.

CHAPTER TWENTY-EIGHT
Mata Hari Delivers Again

EASTGATE MOBILE MANOR, an eclectic collection of '40s and '50s vintage single-wide trailers set on cement blocks, wheels and tires removed long ago. From an aerial view it looked like a random assortment of oversized coffins with windows and awnings in different colors. The property was fenced with only one way in or out.

A light rain began falling as Hitchcock positioned himself outside, on one side of the exit, Walker on the other.

Sergeant Breen pulled the collar of his uniform jacket up as he waited at a pay phone in front of the Eastgate Safeway store, he shivered as he waited. He grabbed the receiver on the first ring.

"Jack? Stan Jurgens here. Whatchya got?"

"We're staking out two armed felons at the Eastgate Mobile Manor. Hitchcock's snitch says they're in the trailer Tyrone Guyon used but we don't know which one it is."

"I remember it well. Light-yellow, the number nineteen is posted next to the door," Jurgens replied.

"We've got 'em staked out. If we can't catch 'em leaving, we'll need a warrant to drag 'em out of there."

"I'm on my way in," Jurgens said.

SERGEANT BREEN MET Hitchcock and Walker outside the trailer park. "The dicks are getting a search warrant for trailer number nineteen. It's yellow."

"I've never worked with a SWAT unit before," Hitchcock said.

"Me either," Breen said. "They'll tell us where they want us when they get here."

"We could have taken those two by ourselves by now. You know that, Jack."

"Ain't that the truth. But we're in a new era of specialization, Roger. So, until the specialists arrive, we generalists will position ourselves and stand by."

Breen turned to Walker. "Ira, go into the trailer park, veer to the right onto the east driveway, find the trailer and set up in a hidden position behind it," Breen ordered. "If the Cadillac is there, let me know, then keep your eyes on it. If they leave, radio me and follow them out. When they're a safe distance from the trailer park, Roger will block them in front. As soon as they've been stopped and can't get away, we'll arrest 'em."

Walker left, leaving Breen and Hitchcock outside the trailer park entrance. Two minutes later, he radioed Breen: *"Got the trailer and suspect vehicle in view."*

As if to oblige what would happen next, the rain stopped.

Walker on the air again: *"Two NMA's are leaving the trailer and entering the suspect vehicle."*

"Follow 'em out," Breen ordered. "Wait for my signal to make the stop. Stay close behind to block their escape."

"Received," Walker replied.

Breen keyed his mic again. "Three Zero Six, when I signal, get in front of the suspect vehicle, block it with yours, then exit and face them, shotgun in hand."

"Ten-Four," Hitchcock acknowledged as he pushed the button under the dash to release his shotgun from the rack.

The white Cadillac Fleetwood appeared. When it had gone about a block from the trailer park, Breen radioed "Now!"

The Cadillac stopped abruptly when Walker flipped the switch of his red light. Hitchcock lit up his overhead light, sped past the Cadillac on the driver side, turned hard right and stopped, blocking the Caddy with the passenger side of his cruiser.

Hitchcock bailed out, shotgun in hand, using his cruiser as a barricade.

Sergeant Breen approached the driver side of the

Cadillac on foot, shotgun at the shoulder.

"Police Department! You are under arrest!" Breen shouted. "Driver—lower your window! Turn off your engine! Throw the keys to the ground! Step out slowly, keep your hands where we can see them. Passenger— place your—"

The driver rammed the passenger side of Hitchcock's patrol car with a loud crash, rocking the cruiser, crushing both doors. A deafening screech of metal followed as it backed up and crushed the grille of Walker's cruiser, bursting the radiator. Hitchcock stepped back as the Cadillac slammed his patrol car a second time.

A deafening boom and a long orange-blue flame from the barrel of Sergeant Breen's shotgun shredded the left front tire. A loud *whoosh* of escaping air followed the blast.

The driver continued ramming the patrol cars behind and in front of him, despite one flat tire, shifting between forward and reverse gears, pulverizing Hitchcock's and Walker's patrol cars in an effort to clear a path of escape.

Walker bailed out of his cruiser before the Cadillac could ram it again.

Breen jacked another round into the chamber of his shotgun and fired into the hood of the Cadillac. Another long plume of orange-blue flame and nine .33 caliber lead balls traveling at over twelve-hundred feet per second tore through the hood of the Cadillac as if it was a sheet of typing paper, instantly killing the motor.

Sergeant Breen racked the action again and aimed through the windshield at the driver. The acrid smells of gunpowder and hot antifreeze puddling on the wet pavement filled the air.

"I'm-a comin' out! Don't shoot!" the passenger shouted as he laid both hands upon the dash, palms up.

Breen kept his shotgun aimed at the driver through the driver door window. The driver solemnly shook his head as he placed his hands on the dash, palms up, and bowed his head in surrender. Breen nodded at Walker, who opened the passenger door, aiming his revolver at the passenger's head.

"Hands behind your head, fingers interlocked, slide out slowly and lay face-down on the ground," Walker ordered in a calm voice.

A huge man, six-foot-three or taller, easily three hundred pounds, young, shaved head, baby-faced, dark-complexioned, as Gayle described, exited the car and laid face-down on the glistening wet pavement. Walker holstered his weapon, cuffed the suspect and removed a full-size chrome-plated revolver from his waistband. Walker helped him to his feet and moved him away from the Cadillac.

"What's your name?" Walker asked.

"Leroy. Leroy Mack."

Walker read the suspect Miranda Rights and

Warnings to him. "Mr. Mack, again, you are under arrest for Unlawful Carrying of a Concealed Weapon. Do you understand these rights?"

"Yes sir, I do," Mack replied, his voice shaking.

"Any more weapons on you?" Walker asked.

"No, sir," he replied, still shaking.

"Okay fine. Do you have any contraband on you?"

"Yes, sir. A little coke in my inside jacket pocket."

Walker removed a plastic baggie containing maybe two ounces of white powder. "Is this what you referred to? Is this cocaine?"

The big man nodded.

Walker seated Mack in the back of his disabled cruiser.

Sergeant Breen nodded at Hitchcock as he kept his shotgun aimed at the driver. "Take him into custody, Roger."

Hitchcock secured his shotgun in his patrol car, opened the driver door of the Cadillac, where the driver still had his hands on the dash, palms up, his forehead on the steering wheel.

"Hands behind your head, interlock your fingers." Hitchcock took hold of his fingers.

"Step out slowly, then turn and face the car."

The driver stepped out and turned to face the Cadillac. Hitchcock moved his left hand from behind his head to behind his back, clicked a handcuff on the driver's left wrist, then repeated the process with the right hand. He patted him down for weapons, finding none. The Washington driver's license in his wallet identified him as Ronald Davis. He refused to talk when Hitchcock read him his Miranda warnings.

Walker held Davis by the handcuffs while Hitchcock searched the Cadillac. Davis began fidgeting when he watched Hitchcock remove a blued Model 1911 .45 automatic pistol and a clear plastic bag containing what appeared to be about three pounds of white powder from under the driver seat. He held it up to Davis' face.

"Want to explain this?"

Davis turned his head and said nothing.

The action was over by the time Delstra's TAG team and two detectives arrived. Two other units arrived to transport the prisoners separately to the station. Walker's patrol car and the Cadillac were towed away and Walker rode in Sergeant Breen's cruiser to the station.

† † †

A FEW MINUTES after 4:00 a.m. Hitchcock called Gayle Warren.

"Hello?" she answered in a sleepy voice.

"Bingo again, Mata," Hitchcock announced. "Thanks to you, we got Davis and the guy with him last night with guns and several pounds of what looks like heroin. Both had outstanding warrants in addition to the new charges they racked up this morning. They won't be going anywhere for a long time."

"Wow, Roger. Nobody got hurt?"

"No one hurt."

"I'm so glad," she said. "Will I get to see you soon?"

"Tomorrow or the next day, for sure."

Hitchcock reflected on Gayle as he hung up. In spite of himself, he was becoming increasingly attracted to her. Besides her physical attributes, her skill as a spy, an informant, added to her mystique.

CHAPTER TWENTY-NINE
The Wackiest Season Of All

PEOPLE SPEND MORE than they have during the holidays. Social pressures often lead otherwise law-abiding people to ruin their spotless records when they celebrate too much, get behind the wheel, get a caught by a store detective in a case of sticky fingers or do other things they wouldn't want to tell a spouse, a judge or a jury.

Prosecutors dread the holidays because the law-abiding folks increase their caseloads with embarrassing matters. This class of offenders try to sweep their misdeeds under the rug by paying their fines promptly and quietly, which boosts the conviction rates just before year's end. A sweet deal for city revenue.

The holidays are also when gangs of professional shoplifters, the ones officers read about in *The Western States Crime Conference* bulletins, seem to materialize in Bellevue every December. The best of the professionals targeted the Frederick & Nelson and the Nordstrom Best stores in Bellevue Square for their higher-end merchandise. They often met their match in the house detectives of either store. Well-regarded by Bellevue cops, case histories of young store detectives were replete with tales of tenacity and derring-do in the face of assault and deadly danger in arresting criminals trying to escape arrest and recovering stolen property.

Restaurants experience an increase in customers skipping out after a meal. Employees chase after customers to get them to either return and pay, or get the license number of the car they left in. Nicknamed "dine n' dash" or "shoe-leather express" by dispatchers, the calls made for easy work for street cops.

The high cash flow of the season made December the most dangerous month for armored car companies. Only a few daring professional stickup men will risk a confrontation with trained armed guards, but when they did, running gun battles in crowded shopping mall parking lots made colorful stories on the evening news.

Career advancement opportunities come up for young criminals. It's a test of nerve for an inexperienced kid to point a loaded gun at another person and demand money. There'd be no turning back if the first robbery was successful. More money with less effort. The very act packs more thrill than burglary, and the recognition and respect from peers which follow all daring deeds, whether good or bad, is a reward in itself.

This year, Charles "Chuck" Dolan, an experienced burglar at age fifteen from the east side of town, decided to try his hand at armed robbery. His decision was influenced by having a .38 revolver and ammunition he stole while on one of his capers. Chuck had been burgling homes since age thirteen. All the cops knew him, and in spite of themselves, they held a liking and a grudging respect for Chuck. He researched and planned his burglaries, which he executed with professional smoothness for someone his age. He learned from his mistakes when they resulted in arrest and always treated arresting officers with genuine respect.

Unlike his scruffy peers, Chuck looked like he stepped out of an Ozzie and Harriet 1950s TV episode. Traditional haircut, slender, always dressed nicely in clean, pressed clothes. Almost any mom would welcome a fine, nice-looking, well-mannered young man like Chuck dating her daughter.

Chuck packed a stolen blued .38 Special revolver with four-inch barrel everywhere he went. Lacking access to the woods or a gun range, he had never fired it. Nevertheless, Chuck was ready to take the leap. Cashflow everywhere was at flood stage. He decided to see if he had the nerve to move up to robbery.

For the past couple early evenings, Chuck hid in the trees across the street, studying his target, the Kwik 'n Cleaners, a laundry and dry cleaners located in a strip mall north of Crossroads on 156th Avenue, a busy thoroughfare.

Early on a Thursday night, Chuck resolved to make his move. The evening cash intake from customers picking up their laundry would be heavy on a Thursday just before a holiday weekend.

The stolen .38 in his jacket pocket, Chuck waited and watched from his hiding place. It began pouring rain, and it was dark. Crossing the street now would be risky because of the poor lighting and heavy rush hour traffic. A dozen customers stood in line at the cash register. He discerned from their movements that almost every one paid in cash.

The slack moment at the cash register in which he would make his move never came. Rain soaked his clothes and he felt chilled. Now or never. He stifled the urge to sneeze—it simply wouldn't do to catch cold on his debut robbery!

Chuck dodged between moving cars across the street. He got in line at the cash register. He watched as everyone ahead of him gave their name, received their clean clothes and paid in cash. By now there must be at least a thousand dollars in the till!

The line moved slowly. It stopped several times when employees searched for the clothes of the waiting customer. Chuck began daydreaming about what he would buy with all the money in the till, when suddenly—

"Name please?" called out the cheerful Asian girl at

the cash register.

"Name please, sir?" she asked, smiling at Chuck.

Suddenly Chuck came to. "Oh! Uh, Chuck! I-I mean Charles—Charles Dolan!" he blurted reactively. He shook his head when he remembered his mission. "Hey, wait! No! Don't check for my clothes. I've got a gun! Give me all the money in the till!"

The girl behind the cash register smiled a big-sister smile and laughed good-naturedly. "C'mon! You don't have a gun. You look like a nice boy."

"I'll show you I'm not such a nice boy," he blurted as he gripped the gun in his jacket pocket and pulled. The gun's hammer snagged on the inside lining of his pocket. After tugging several times Chuck finally got it out, ripping the pocket. Lint was on the gun and his hand shook as he pointed it at the girl.

"See? I do have a gun! Now hand over all the money and be quick!"

The girl stopped smiling and handed all the cash to Chuck, which he stuffed into his jacket pocket as he ran past the line of customers and out the door.

Otis happened to be a block away when the call came in. It would be the first and only armed robbery call of his career in which the victim and witnesses were laughing hysterically when he arrived. Otis couldn't help but laugh too when he heard the story. He knew Chuck from arresting him as a juvenile. Within an hour he had the money, the gun, and Chuck, in custody.

† † †

ON THE WEST side of town at the same time, in the parking lot of the closed Midlakes Chevron station at the corner of NE 8th Street and 116th Avenue, Officer Lee Wooten pulled over a battered green Ford pickup for weaving in his travel lane. He noticed an Out West taxi cab parked in the parking lot, lights out, driver behind the wheel, as he exited his cruiser and walked up to the driver door of the pickup.

The taxi driver, his attention drawn by Wooten's flashing red light, glanced at Wooten then quickly lowered his gaze.

Wooten, formerly a Montana cowboy until he served on Navy swift boats in Vietnam, was built in the fashion of a heavyweight wrestler. Flashlight in his left hand, Wooten contacted the driver in the pickup. He smelled alcohol on the driver's breath as soon as he rolled his window down. The driver's eyes were red and watery. He stared at Wooten as if dazed.

"Evening sir," Wooten began. "The reason I pulled you over is because I noticed you crossing out of your lane three times in the last quarter mile of so. Have you been drinking, sir?"

The driver stared at Wooten as he nodded once but said nothing.

"Show me your driver's license, sir."

No response. The driver started at Wooten as if in a drunken stupor.

Wooten opened the driver door. "Please step out of your vehicle, sir."

The driver, a workman type, broad-shouldered, lean and muscular, stumbled when trying to walk heel-to-toe in a straight line, the first of the routine physical sobriety tests. He couldn't touch his fingers to his nose while standing with his feet together. He got as far as the letter m in reciting the alphabet.

"You're under arrest for driving while intoxicated," Wooten said. The man threw a punch when Wooten reached for his arm. Wooten deflected the blow and struck back, hitting the man on the side of the head. They stood toe-to-toe, trading hard punches, each connecting with a resounding thud that rocked the other. The man yelled unintelligibly as he threw punches. Wooten's blows were many, hard, and accurate, his only words, "You're under arrest!"

When the suspect threw a roundhouse punch, Wooten seized his arm and powered him to the asphalt. The man rolled over when Wooten tried to handcuff him, kicking him twice, knocking him back each time. The suspect got up, bent from the waist and charged, screaming like an enraged bear.

Wooten stepped aside just in time. The suspect crashed head-first into the rear door of the police cruiser. He fell back, stunned from the impact. Wooten stood him up and tried again to handcuff him.

The suspect kicked and swung wild punches.

Wooten slammed him head first into the rear door of the patrol car twice, denting it. The suspect collapsed to the ground. The driver struggled to get back on his feet, but was too delirious to stand. He sat back down on the asphalt.

Wooten clicked the handcuffs on and opened the rear door of his patrol car.

Two carloads of teenagers waiting at the traffic signal on NE 8th Street rolled down their windows and honked their horns and cheered, "Hey, yeah! Get the pig!" as the man wobbled to his feet and head-butted Wooten. Both men were gasping for air. Wooten, still in the fight, seized the suspect by the handcuffs behind his back and lifted up, bending the suspect at the waist, and rammed him into the rear seat and slammed the door.

At that moment Otis arrived.

"Radio sent me to check on you when you didn't call back on the air. Looks like you got it under control," he said.

"I'm okay," Wooten said, grinning as he recovered his breath. "I'm gonna have to quit smokin' if I gotta do this again," he said between breaths. "Got a little scuffed up getting this guy into custody for DWI. He's a roofer by trade. Strongest guy I've ever fought. If he weren't drunk, I don't know if I could have taken him."

The suspect was hollering to be set free. He started kicking the door and window with both feet. Wooten asked Otis, "Would you mind standing by for the impound of his truck?"

"Glad to," Otis replied, "but first let's keep him from kicking your car apart even more than it already is."

Wooten and Otis fought the man back out of the car, placed restraints on his feet and removed his boots while he tried to kick them. They fought him back into Wooten's dented patrol car.

Otis chuckled as Wooten shut the door. "You needed this, didn't you?"

Wooten laughed. "You mean after the Village Inn fight? You bet I did! I feel great! Thanks." Before Wooten left for the station, the cab driver, Hakimian walked over to him, smiling ear-to-ear.

"Hey, officer. I tell you something," Hakimian said in broken, accented English. "I see what happen. From now on, if Bellevue officer tell me 'do this, do that,' I salute and say 'yes, *sir!*'" Hakimian snapped a salute.

Wooten laughed again as he fastened his seat belt. "Thanks! I appreciate it." He turned around in his seat as he put his gear in drive. "Hold on, buddy, the station is just a few blocks from here. Three hots and a cot are waitin' for ya!"

CHAPTER THIRTY
Minding The Three B's

IN A WINDOW SEAT at Snoqualmie Falls Lodge they sat, over-looking tons of white, cascading waters falling ninety feet to an aquamarine pool, surrounded by cedars and Douglas fir trees within feet of the water's edge, set the stage. Day or night, the radiant white mist rising to the top of the waterfall created the atmosphere of mystery and romance the Falls were famous for.

Hitchcock couldn't help but notice that as modestly as Gayle dressed, her primal appeal shone through. Despite their scenic viewpoint, she picked at her food, saying nothing throughout the three-course meal.

"You're awfully quiet," he remarked when the waiter brought coffee and dessert. "Is something wrong?"

She smiled shyly. "Oh, nothing much. Just thinking."

"Uh-oh," he said, only half-joking.

Gayle set her fork down and turned to face him. "I'm thinking about us. Is there an 'us,' in the future, Roger?"

Inwardly he shook his head as he stared at his plate and pushed the food around with his fork. *Here she goes again. Every time I'm with her, she pushes for what I can't give her. I want to, but I can't risk a romance with her. Not only is she a paid informant, there will always be the worry she'd eventually return to heroin and her old life. With each arrest she sets up, she increases the pressure to move the relationship forward. Broads, booze and bucks—broads, booze and bucks, the policeman's downfall, Ira keeps telling me. Besides, there are details about her past she doesn't want me to know about...*

And yet, without saying a word or even looking at her, he felt himself weakening. *How not? Just look at her. How long before I cave in? We're both single and unattached,* he rationalized. *Why not? Where's the harm?*

When they arrived at her apartment, he shut the engine off and collected his thoughts. *Should I go in with her?* Mentally he shook his head. *A beautiful girl, put together like she is, works in a bar where lots of men go, never married, no kids, yet no boyfriends? It doesn't compute.*

"I want to ask you if—" He stopped when a carload of rowdy college kids parked next to them and noisily piled out and headed for one of the second-floor apartments.

"What?" she asked snappishly.

With a look which said *until next time*, he gave her an envelope containing two hundred dollars. Without a word she sprang upon him, kissed him forcefully on the lips, then bolted out, slamming the door so hard the window shook.

He watched her run to her apartment and slam the door. *She isn't in this for the money—she wants me. And I haven't made the advances toward her men usually make. As attractive as she is, something besides Walker's advice keeps me from crossing the line. I could play it safe and end it, but Gayle's work is too valuable—she is saving young lives, still willing to take huge personal risks. After the loss of Ruby, I'm an emotional mannikin.* He shook his head again. *I'm playing with fire. If I give in once, there's no return. I should turn her over to the Seattle or the federal narcs to work with them—but I can't let her go.*

CHAPTER THIRTY-ONE
The Telltale Party

RHONDA'S LOG HOME, decorated for Christmas inside and out, included a sprig of mistletoe hanging over the front door. Her guests were all doctors and nurses, except for Hitchcock. He felt someone's eyes on him. He turned around. Across the living room a slender young doctor, drink in hand, glared at him with open hatred. Puzzled, Hitchcock approached him and extended his hand. "Hi. I'm Roger." The young doc's face reddened as he walked away.

"What do you do on the police department?" a pale, frazzled-looking woman doctor, as featureless as the green olive floating in her martini asked. She appeared to be in her late thirties.

"We respond to calls of all kinds, take reports, and make arrests, mostly," he replied casually.

"What do you do when there are no calls?"

"Patrol the streets for suspicious people and

situations."

"Ooh. *That* sounds *boring* and monotonous," she sniffed. "How much do you get paid to do *that*?"

He smiled politely and moved on.

A paunchy physician in his fifties with thinning gray hair and a bushy mustache came up from behind Hitchcock and slapped him on the back.

"I hear you're one of Bellevue's finest!"

He nodded.

"Do you know Bill Harris on your Department?" he bellowed without introducing himself.

"Sure do."

"Harris is a motor cop, a sergeant now. I used to buy him coffee whenever I saw him at a restaurant. I bet you can't guess what he did to me after he became sergeant."

"No, but I have a feeling you're going to tell me."

"Ha-ha-ha! Funny man here!" the fat doc roared. "Well, let me tell you! Harris was sitting on his motorcycle at NE 8th and 116th, and when he recognized my car, zoom! He gave me a ticket for running the red light! What a jerk! After all the coffee I sprung for! I went to court, of course, and guess what happened?"

"The judge and the chief are your golfing buddies, so the laws don't apply to you and you got off scot-free."

"Hah! Funny man again! Nope!" he exclaimed, a spray of spittle landed on Hitchcock. "I wish! I *do* play golf with Sean Carter, that's *Chief* Carter to you, my boy! As I was saying, that *bastard* Harris lied in court and

Judge Hadley believed him over me! They were in cahoots with each other, I tell—"

Hitchcock turned his back on him mid-sentence and stepped outside to the back yard. Rhonda followed.

"I'm really sorry, and embarrassed for the way some of my associates are behaving, babe. I'll make it up to you tonight," she promised, with a wink and a kiss on the lips.

A man's voice came from the shadows. "Yeah, yeah, yeah. Let's hear it for the hero-cop we read about in the papers. Boxing champ, war hero, killer of criminals, blah-blah-blah!"

The young doctor who wouldn't shake his hand emerged from the shadows of the shrubbery. Scowling, he wobbled across the lawn toward Hitchcock.

"Shtand ashide, Rhonda, I'll show you what your *hero* is all about," he said, his words thickened by alcohol.

Rhonda stayed next to Hitchcock. "Howard, stop! Roger is my guest!"

"C'mon *Roger*, Howard said in a mocking tone. "Let's go a round or two, right here!" He put his fists up and stood, swaying, moving his fists in a milling motion. "C'mon, fight," he loudly slurred.

Hitchcock put his hands into his slacks pockets and stepped away from Rhonda. "No, you're *way* too tough for me," he replied, deftly side-stepping Howard's wild punches.

Howard screamed obscenities when he almost fell and his best punches missed Hitchcock. "Shtand still and fight!" he bellowed.

Other guests came out of the house, drinks in their hands, smiling and commenting amusedly like they came to watch a tennis match on the lawn.

"Howard, stop! You're drunk and acting like a fool!" Rhonda shouted, her face contorted with anger.

But Howard, drunk as he was, would have none of it. He spewed curses, personal insults and threats at Hitchcock. Lunging clumsily, he threw more punches with all his strength but never touched Hitchcock, who never took his hands out of his pockets.

The guests sipped their drinks and snickered at their colleague, now face-down on the grass, winded, too drunk to get up on his own. Hitchcock extended his hand to help him up. "It's okay, Howard, no hard feelings." But Howard swatted Hitchcock's hand away, loudly cursing him again.

Hitchcock strode purposefully around the house to his car. Rhonda ran after him. "Roger, please forgive me! I'm so sorry! I had no idea they were like this. And Howard, I never thought—"

"Howard's a drunken souse, and he's jealous," he said as he fired up his El Camino. "This isn't your fault, Rhonda, it's reality. Even if I became a doctor, I'd never fit in with people like them, nor would I want to."

Rhonda hung on the driver door with both hands,

crying as he began backing out. "Don't leave! I'll send them all away," she pleaded.

Hitchcock shook his head. "These are your people. They're your world," he replied kindly, "but thanks for the invite."

In his rearview mirror was Rhonda standing in her driveway, dejected. An unexpected peace, a sense of release came over him. He understood his true social standing. Until tonight he had wondered whether he had a sense of place with Rhonda; no more. He understood and accepted the social isolation that came with the badge, the blue, the eight-point billed hat, the .38 Special.

Time to move on, soldier.

CHAPTER THIRTY-TWO
Allie

HE FELT RESTED when he awoke, filled with the peace of knowing where the road of life *wouldn't* be taking him. A morning run with Jamie cleared his thinking. He showered, dressed, and headed for the Pancake Corral.

Jane, one of the owner's daughters, seated him in Allie's section as soon as he walked in. "Allie'll be here in a sec," she said, handing him the morning *Post Intelligencer*, which he started to pretend reading when he heard a familiar voice.

"Hi Roger. We missed you this past week. How was your time away?" Allie asked as she poured his coffee.

He paused to consider his answer. *If I say I worked outdoors repairing fences on a ranch, killed coyotes and wolves and helped nail some cattle rustlers, she'd either laugh in my face or get mad at me for lying*, he mused good-naturedly. But then he felt encouraged when she said, "We missed you."

"Thanks. I got my batteries recharged by getting away for a couple weeks, but I'm glad to be back," he replied, puzzled by the reservation in her eyes.

Allie set the coffee pot down, got her order pad and pencil out, and stared at him, waiting.

"Buckwheats and bacon again?"

He pretended indecision to keep her standing next to him a little longer. "Uh, hmm. Ah, nope," he said after as long a delay as he could manage. "Looks like potato pancakes, poached eggs and sausage patties today."

She wrote up the order and left without a word, which worried him.

As he peeked over the newspaper at Allie waiting on customers, absorbing her natural charm, hearing the femininity in her voice, the womanly rhythm in her movements, Bill Chace, the owner of the Corral, pulled up a chair.

"How ya doin,' Hitch?" he asked with a friendly grin. "You've been away for a while. I bet you needed a break after all the action you've been in."

"I love this town, Bill," Hitchcock replied, setting the newspaper down, "but I needed a change of scenery. I'm glad to be back."

"Your mom came here with one of your sisters. Sorry but I can't tell the twins apart," Bill remarked.

"Must've been Jean. She's single and often goes places with Mom. Joan's married, has a baby and another in the oven."

His eyes followed Allie as he and Bill chatted. Seeing this, Bill leaned forward. "I'm not one to stick my nose in somebody else's business, Hitch," he said in a low voice, "but I'm not so old I can't see what's going You're not the only good lookin' guy who comes here just to see Allie. She won't be available forever. Man-to-man, I advise strikin' while the iron's hot."

Hitchcock nodded thanks. Bill left to tend to other customers. When Allie brought his order, he said "I hope you'll forgive me for such short notice, but I'd like to take you out tonight. Dinner and a movie, if you're available."

She studied him for several seconds. "I need a sitter for my son. I'm off at two. Call me at about three."

"I'll call you at three. Call your mom."

"You know I don't date," she reminded him.

"Call your mom," he reminded her.

CHAPTER THIRTY-THREE
The Date

FOR THE REST of her shift Allie was almost too nervous to keep working. Her phone rang at exactly three. Heart in her throat, she told him her mom agreed to babysit. "Pick you up at five," he said…didn't he? Her mind was aflutter—*shower and shampoo, yes, then makeup, hair, nails, and oh, what to wear?*

At five o'clock sharp he was at her door. He couldn't help looking her up and down before he could say a word. Dressed in a black wool sweater-dress which set off her hourglass figure and ivory complexion, square-toed platform boots, pearl necklace, blonde tresses, she was perfect.

She introduced him to her mother.

"I remember you," she said.

"Yes, I remember seeing you too, Ma'am. In the parking lot a little while back."

Agnes nodded. "That strange rumpled old man with the camera—who was he?"

"A private eye paid to spy on Allie, Mrs. Malloy. He wouldn't tell me who his client was."

"Who else but the McAuliffes!" Agnes snorted with disgust. "But never mind that. Thanks for getting Allie out for a few hours. All she does is take care of her son and work. She's going back to college part time this coming winter quarter. She's too young for such a life."

Allie blushed. "Please, Mom."

He helped her into her camel overcoat and took her gently by the arm. "We're going to dinner and a movie a few minutes from here, in the Square. We'll call before the movie to see if Trevor is all right."

She smiled to herself when he opened the passenger door of his El Camino for her. "Hope you like Chinese," he said as he started the engine. "I reserved a private room for us at the Mandarin."

"Chinese is good," she said.

The Mandarin, a carpeted, white-tablecloth, linen napkin kind of place, managed to maintain a hushed atmosphere even though its cocktail lounge was a favorite watering hole for rowdy local car salesmen. They ordered a combination dinner for two and talked through the meal, avoiding mention of the mysterious "Jim Reynolds" or her former in-laws.

"Which movie are we seeing?" she asked.

"The newest release, *Patton*, a war movie starring

George C. Scott."

"I thought you'd want to see the new Clint Eastwood movie, it's a western."

"We'll see it next. Now that we're finished, let's call your mom to check on Trevor. If all is well, show time is in thirty minutes," he said as he fished cash out of his wallet.

THE BEL-VUE THEATER in Bellevue Square was typical of the movie houses of the late '40s. A plush maroon and green floral pattern carpet covered the lobby and the stairs to the balcony. Upstairs were the higher priced loge seats, deep and luxurious, on the other side of heavy velvet maroon curtains, perfect for smoochers.

"Two seats, loge section" he told the young girl in the ticket booth.

"Which loge section, sir?" she asked. "Upstairs in the balcony or downstairs."

About this he didn't need to think. "Upstairs," he replied.

The two rows of seats were empty. Allie followed him to the back row so no one could sit behind them. The stage was set. She did her best to relax, but her body tingled with desire and excitement at being next to him. *Let whatever happens next, happen,* she thought, hardly believing she was with the man who so dominated her thoughts.

On the screen, George C. Scott, in Army dress uniform, strutted onstage as General Patton to address his men. A huge American flag covered the wall behind him as he gave a motivating speech. Hitchcock heard the phrase "*Americans love to fight*" as Allie sat motionless next to him, absorbing his presence, staring at the screen but not seeing the movie.

He touched her wrist after the first battle scene to ask if he could get her anything from downstairs. She put her other hand on his and turned toward him. He took her in his arms and as their lips met, a fire, pent up for months, burst into flame, and burned hot for the next two hours. Fortunately, no one else came up to the loge section.

Their mussed clothes and hair drew grins from the other patrons as they passed through the lobby after the movie. He opened the door of his El Camino for her. She slipped her arms around him as soon as he got in and the passion raged again. They ignored other movie-goers who stared at them as they got into their cars next to Hitchcock's.

The windows fogged over as they kissed with fierce hunger. "We've got to stop," she panted, sitting back.

"Why? Why stop?" he asked, his voice husky with emotion, leaning after her in pursuit, kissing her neck.

"I'm not like what you're probably thinking," she replied, pushing him back to look at him better.

"What do you mean?"

"I'm not careless about love like so many people are today. I was a virgin when Glendon got me pregnant. I told you how short my marriage to him was, and why. I haven't been out with anyone since he left me," Allie said, still catching her breath.

He touched her arm. She touched his, then stopped.

"Please take me home before I lose control of myself. If there's anything to this, I want it to be right."

It pleased and surprised him to meet someone so beautiful who put a high standard on her affections. He started the car without another word and arrived at her apartment in minutes. He opened the passenger door and walked her up the stairs.

"Don't misunderstand me, Roger," she said when they reached the top step. "I accepted my feelings for you when I learned someone tried to kill you. I not only accept those feelings, I welcome them. I just don't want to make any more mistakes. As a mom, I must put my son ahead of myself."

"Can I kiss you one more time before I go?" he asked, putting his hands gently on her shoulders, his insides burning with passion. She nodded slightly, and once more their lips met.

Allie went to bed a changed woman. Thoughts of Hitchcock filled her mind. The intensity of her feelings for him surprised her. Her plans to remain single to raise her son had vanished like smoke. She wanted this man. She faced her need for him when she learned two criminals tried to kill him. Now that her love for him was out in the open, it had an intensity she never knew before, and it frightened her.

Hitchcock went home a changed man. Thoughts of Allie consumed him. He brought Jamie inside and built a fire. Coffee wouldn't do tonight, he wanted whiskey – the proper drink for American men, in his opinion. For the first time in a while, he got out his guitar, and played as he relived his evening with her. He could still feel his arms around her and taste her lips.

MEANWHILE, ACROSS TOWN, two other Department members met in secret for what would become a defining meeting for many, especially Hitchcock.

CHAPTER THIRTY-FOUR
Fireside Confidential

THE SECRET MEETING happened in the rustic hunting lodge atmosphere of a meeting room at Clinkerdagger, Bickerstaff and Pett's, a pricey, colonial-style restaurant on the shore of Lake Bellevue, where waiters and waitresses wore period correct Colonial era costumes.

Both men were in their mid-thirties, the prime of life. Accomplished and well-groomed, their upward career paths paralleled each other. They sat in mutual silence at first, to allow a settling-in before they tackled the important matters that caused them to meet.

Expensive, pleated gabardine slacks, cashmere sweaters, and polished loafers, they lounged in brown brocade wing-back chairs, sipping fine whiskey, staring at the hissing orange and blue flames licking the ceramic logs of the gas fireplace.

"Where should we start? My guess is our little lieutenant friend," Captain Delstra asked, breaking the silence.

The captain of detectives, Dennis Holland, nodded and smacked his lips as he sipped his whiskey. "Ah, yes, the mysterious, treacherous Bostwick, who doesn't realize he handed us his head on a platter by leaving his secret memos where Jack Breen found them."

"Not yet, he doesn't," Delstra said as he stared into the fire, contemplatively stroking his mustache. "I'm not religious, but the way Bostwick inadvertently left those memos on his desk and the way Breen happened to find them is nothing short of divine timing."

"But other than the intern he wrote to, we don't know who gives Bostwick his orders."

Delstra crossed one leg over the other. "Not yet, we don't."

"The Department loses if we don't play our hand well," Holland said ruefully.

"The mistakes won't be ours."

"How can you be so sure?" Holland asked.

"I have inside sources. To change the subject for a second, I want to brag a bit."

Holland nodded the go-ahead as he took another sip of his whiskey.

"The two who died in the shooting picked the worst officers to attack. Almost like they had a subconscious death wish," Delstra said.

Holland nodded in agreement and chuckled. "The stuff of action movies, except it was real."

"I re-read their files after it happened," Delstra said. "They had both killed in combat more than once, which explains why they didn't panic."

"They made no mistakes, that's for sure," Holland agreed.

"When the crooks opened fire on 'em they held their ground and went straight to their guns. Now two of the worst criminals we've ever had are pushing up daisies."

"Yeah, and *you* did right by them, Erik, and the rest of the Department by letting the Coroner's Office handle the inquiry."

"I had no choice when I found out the third-floor faction was bent on crucifying them no matter how justified they were."

Holland paused, gazing at the fire. "It was a bold move, depriving city management, like snatching meat from a lion," he observed. "As shootings go, it was textbook perfect. Morale is up and the public has a new respect for us. The city is safer."

"There's another side to it, Dennis," Delstra said.

"There is?"

"If the officers hadn't been veterans with combat experience who practice on their own, we'd be trying to live with a very opposite outcome."

"I think I know where you're going with this, but go on," Holland said.

"I'm frustrated," Delstra confided. "We haven't been able to train or qualify for four years now since the

City Manager closed our range. The killing of four Highway Patrol officers by two armed felons on a robbery spree in Newhall last spring should have made enough of an impression on our Chief that he'd push for a new range, but he did nothing."

"You talked to him about it. What did he say?" Holland asked.

Delstra snorted. "All Sean said was, 'Well that's California, it'll never happen here.' A few months later, when the same thing did happen here but with a better outcome, I spoke to him again."

"And?"

"He took the position that it was a freak incident which wouldn't happen again."

"Did you say anything else?" Holland asked.

"You know me, Dennis. I told Sean what he already knew, that our guys are unqualified and unprepared to be armed. I told him that when the next shooting happens, ACLU lawyers will use the City's negligence to sue the snot out of us, and rightfully so," Delstra said heatedly.

"This is why Sean should retire," Holland nodded. "We came out fine this time, but a bunch of untrained men carrying guns in public, who are expected to use those guns to protect others and overcome criminal elements, is unacceptable. The Chief makes himself a liability for allowing this negligence."

The waitress came with fresh drinks and left.

"Attacks on officers are going up everywhere. We aren't immune," Delstra said. "We not only have to fight to get a range, we have unknown plotters upstairs to deal with. They were about to throw Hitchcock and Sherman to the wolves until I ran interference. They'll have to lay low and lick their wounds until they come up with a new line of attack, as Bostwick's memos confirm."

"A new range isn't all we need," Holland said, glancing at Delstra, then returning his gaze to the fire. "Drugs and organized crime is flourishing everywhere. We need a full-time narcotics unit, and an intelligence team, like Seattle has."

Delstra stared into the fire, frowning. "I'm taking no action on Bostwick until I know who the other players are and what they're next move is."

"Good thing you didn't show Bostwick's memos to the Chief. Sean is so anxious to retire on a high note that the memos would wind up in the hands of the very people who are behind our little lef-tenant."

"I'm giving Hitchcock and Sherman political armor to make them harder targets in the future."

"How so?"

"Service commendations for bravery, awarded publicly, with a notice in the paper. Plus, teaching assignments showing new officers what happens in a deadly situation. A slew of letters from grateful citizens whom I know will appear in the paper and their files."

Holland nodded his approval. "That'll stop anyone

from taking another run at them," he said.

"What escapes me, Dennis, is how Bostwick got promoted twice in record time without doing anything. He's never even made one arrest on his own," Delstra said. "His test scores are always too perfect—like someone gave him the questions ahead of time. He looks down his nose at all of us, and the troops despise him. It doesn't add up—it's bad math."

"Not all of the troops despise him, Erik"

"No?"

"Bostwick has a small following in the ranks."

"Amazing," Delstra muttered.

"He's a mouse in the corner, reporting on us for the third floor and beyond," Holland said.

"Explain."

"What's been going on in Seattle is coming here."

Delstra leaned forward, focused. "That can't be."

"Hear me out," Holland said. "Last January, Chicago Seven defendant Jerry Rubin gave an inflammatory speech here. It inspired the Seattle Liberation Front to organize protests here in anticipation of the verdict against the Chicago Seven. They were jailed along with their attorneys for contempt of court before the jury reached their verdicts.

"After that, Chip Marshall led the Seattle Liberation Front promoted a 'Stop the Courts Day' to shut down the Seattle Federal Courthouse."

Delstra nodded. "I was at the Federal Courthouse,

with our tactical team."

"Yes, you were. In fact, you went against the orders of what I call the third-floor-faction. I'm surprised they didn't demote you."

Delstra shrugged. "We train in an empty church parking lot on our side of Clyde Hill. Apparently the third-floor-folks, whoever they are, never got wind of it, or I'd be selling used cars now instead of talking to you."

"Another miracle," Holland said.

"*Another* miracle?"

"The way the shooting went down is the first."

"Ah," Delstra said, smirking. "True. After they found out we assisted Seattle twice in the riots over there, I was told in writing to disband the unit."

"What did you do? The squad is still intact."

Delstra shrugged and sipped his whiskey. "I didn't see the Chief's name on it. The signature was unreadable and unfamiliar, probably one of those young Bolshevik interns from the University."

"Then what happened?"

Delstra shook his head. "I *can't* remember what I did with the letter..."

Holland finished his whiskey and set the glass down. "Radicals are gaining ground because they are more committed to their cause than the average working, family-raising guy. So the public slumbers like sheep huddled in a pen while the radicals gain control in gradual steps," he said. "The core values that define us are being trampled, violent crime is up and a new breed of criminals consider ambushing cops a virtue. Traditional criminals like Colin Wilcox are a dying breed. What happened to him proves organized crime is not only changing, it's taking over the hippie drug craze and is moving into the suburbs. Yet, nobody does or says anything."

"*Has* moved in, actually," Delstra corrected.

"The new breed of criminals is organized and radically politicized. The means justifies the ends. SPD Intelligence uncovered the evidence that led to the indictments of the 'Seattle Eight' for instigating and leading the attack on the Federal Courthouse. Now they're targeting the SPD itself."

"Damn," Delstra mumbled, shifting in his seat.

"Their investigation exposed the backers of the anti-war movement. The names would surprise you."

"Such as?"

When Holland mentioned five prominent names. Delstra shook his head. "The days when the local news agencies swarmed all over a house when they found out Gus Hall was there, are gone. I had no idea."

"I remember that" Holland said. "Gus Hall, the head of the American Communist Party, hid himself in a house in the Central District. The whole area was up in arms that a communist leader was visiting here. Those days are gone, Erik."

"Why are they gone—what's changed?"

"Powerful elitists are undermining our values, our way of life, almost unopposed," Holland replied.

Delstra, becoming agitated, said, "I see that, but *why* is there no outrage or even concern?"

"Most people today sit back, minding their own business in thoughtless complacency while our enemies creep in, demanding and getting small changes until it's too late—the same way a few Nazis took over Germany, a few Bolsheviks took Russia," Holland said. "We're set for the unthinkable to happen next."

"What would that be?"

"A home-grown commie gets elected to the Seattle City Council. Then SPD's Intelligence Unit is dissolved, and Chief George Tilsch is replaced by a political hack."

Delstra stroked his mustache as he gazed into the hissing orange and blue gas flames. "A hack like our little lieutenant? God forbid."

"We read the same teletypes," Holland said. "While not much happens here compared to Seattle, that's changing too. The attacks on the symbols of society, like flag burning, are signs of the new trend toward collectivism. Nobody has the guts to call it for what it is—communism under a benign label."

Delstra shifted in his chair again as he digested Holland's revelations.

"The local scandals left us with a leadership vacuum at the worst possible time," Holland said.

"I remember," Delstra said. "The County Prosecutor

lost reelection after a three-year investigation by the Seattle papers linked him to the police payoff system. Similar scandals in the Sheriff's Office resulted in forced resignations, damaging public trust and strengthening the radicals' position."

"Restoring trust will be hard," Delstra commented.

"It'll take strong, clean leaders who aren't afraid to take risks and make enemies. We need you to be our next chief, Erik."

Delstra looked at Holland in surprise.

"What about you? I thought you wanted the job."

"I did, once upon a time. But I'm not that man—you are. You're an ex-Marine, you fought in Korea. The men, especially our young *veteranos* who served in Vietnam, will follow you into Hell itself, and you know it. I'll support you. The troops will form their own bargaining unit, a guild, like Seattle has. They won't go union like the teamsters. When they do, they'll use their influence to defy the City and support you."

Delstra nodded. "I'll need their support."

"I have a prediction to make."

"Do tell," Delstra said after another sip of whiskey.

"College draft-deferments are a big mistake. It makes our colleges a hideout for draft-dodgers instead of places of higher learning. Many will stay in long enough to become professors. They'll justify themselves by claiming the war is immoral. They'll infect future generations with communist ideals, disguised as socialism and teach future generations to hate our country. When the draft ends, the anti-war movement will dissolve, but collectivism will continue."

Delstra paused, thinking. "What you say makes sense, but I hope you're wrong."

"I'm not wrong. In the meantime, you need to become more political."

Delstra turned toward Holland, surprised. "I'm *not* political?"

"You need to be *deliberately* political, in the same sense that your four favorite officers are *deliberate* street cops. It isn't a job to them, it's life."

After what seemed an interminably long pause, Delstra nodded. "I'll take that under advisement, Dennis."

"And while you're at it, hang on to your 'inside source.' She's on her way up and she's gold."

Delstra stared at Holland, stunned. Before he could ask Holland how he knew, Holland held up his hand as he got up to leave.

"Don't ask. I have my sources too."

CHAPTER THIRTY-FIVE
Shadows of the Cell Block

ON SATURDAY NIGHT, the bars and dance places were in full swing by 8:00 p.m. The weather was cold enough for Hitchcock's heavy winter coat. He listened to the steady stream of calls as he rolled out of the station. None of them involved Eastgate. Seeing more than a half-dozen cars parked in front of The Great Wall made him want to stop in for a bar check just to shake things up a bit, but the message from Mata said she needed him at The Wagon Wheel right away.

Boisterous crowds of mostly bowling league couples packed the restaurant and the bar. Despite the holiday mood, Hitchcock detected an ominous tension in Ralph the bartender when he walked in.

He spotted Gayle carrying a tray of drinks to a table, looking luscious in her long-sleeved white blouse and black skirt. Her eyes caught his. Without turning her head or saying anything she motioned with her eyes to the table against the wall across from the far end of the bar where three hard-looking biker types sat, each nursing a drink.

The two facing the door tensed up the second Hitchcock appeared. One of them muttered something to the one sitting with his back to the door, wearing a jeans jacket, lightning bars tattooed on his neck. He hunched forward but didn't turn around.

Hitchcock sauntered up to the bartender as if he didn't notice them. "Another busy night, eh, Ralph?" he commented casually, leaning on the bar, using the back mirror to inspect the three.

"Yep, another bowling tournament tonight," Ralph replied in a clear voice. As he bent down to dunk soapy glasses in rinse water, he warned in a low voice, "The one in the jean jacket's packing a piece in his waistband. He's covered it now, but I saw it—right side."

"After I leave, unlock your back door for me. We'll take it from there," Hitchcock replied softly.

"The coffee's stale or I'd offer you some. I'll be making a fresh pot in an hour or two," Ralph said in a clear voice.

"Great. If I can, I'll be back in about two hours unless I'm on a call," Hitchcock said just loud enough for the men at the table to hear. The second he reached his cruiser, he radioed Walker.

"If you're clear, meet me at The Wagon Wheel right away."

Walker arrived in minutes.

"A robbery might be about to go down in The Wagon Wheel lounge. Three hard biker types are in the bar, keeping to themselves, nursing their drinks, watching everything and everyone. The bartender told me he saw the one wearing a jeans jacket with lightning bars tatted on his neck has a piece tucked in his back waistband."

"Where exactly are they?"

Hitchcock described their position. "Tatted like they are, narcs they're not."

Walker's eyes narrowed as he unsnapped his holster. "Gang members or convicts. Let's shake 'em down."

"Ralph unlocked the back door for us so we'll be on 'em quick," Hitchcock said.

"Ah, yes, the old element-of-surprise trick," Walker said, exuding playful confidence.

They paused at the back door for a second, then burst in, too fast for the first man at the table who saw them to alert his companions. Hitchcock kept his hand on his revolver as he moved toward the men. The bartender, Gayle, and several customers riveted their attention to what would happen next.

Hitchcock leaned down and spoke in the ear of the jean-jacketed one in a low voice as he put his left hand on the man's shoulder to gauge his intentions. "Put your empty hands on the table where we can see 'em. Are you guys armed?"

The men froze, saying nothing.

Walker saw that the hands of the other two men were under the table. He drew his gun and stepped clear of Hitchcock in case it came to shooting. "You two put empty hands on the table where we can see them," he ordered. "If no one is armed, there's no problem."

The man across from the jean-jacketed one froze, staring at Walker's gun, keeping both hands under the table. The other man slowly placed empty hands on the table. The crowd in the lounge gathered by the front door, ready to flee if shooting started, watching.

Walker pressed the business end of his gun against the temple of the man who wouldn't show his hands, and cocked the hammer. Hitchcock took a half-step back and drew his gun, covering the other two men.

"Empty hands on the table, I said," Walker ordered. The man obeyed.

"Where's your piece?" Walker demanded, keeping his gun at the suspect's head.

"In my lap," he replied in a hoarse voice, staring straight ahead.

"Don't move a muscle," Walker warned as he reached under the table with his free hand.

A woman in the crowd gasped when Walker removed a blued revolver from the man's lap and put it into his waistband. "All three of you—hands behind your heads, stand slowly and face the wall," he ordered.

Walker covered Hitchcock as he handcuffed and searched each one. He removed a stainless steel revolver from the waistband of the man in the jeans jacket and a blued 9mm automatic in the waistband of the other man.

A fearful hush fell over the crowd as Hitchcock and Walker marched the handcuffed suspects past them through the front door.

Hitchcock radioed Sergeant Breen, "Contact me and Three Zero Eight at The Wagon Wheel."

A California driver's license identified the man in the jean jacket as Donald G. Cloward, with a date of birth in 1942. Hitchcock ran him through NCIC, the national crime database. While he waited for a response, he read Cloward his Constitutional rights then asked, "Do you understand your rights?"

"Yeah."

"What are you guys doing here, armed, in a bar?"

"Just passing through. What of it? We did nothing wrong. Other than that, I ain't sayin' nothin'."

"How did you get here?"

No answer.

Hitchcock tried another angle. "Where have you done time?"

Cloward shrugged. "You're gonna find out anyway. San Quentin."

"Are you on parole?"

No answer.

"Are you wanted?"

"Phhh!" Cloward snorted. "I ain't doin' your job for ya. You're the Man, do your own work."

SERGEANT BREEN ARRIVED. Walker seated the third prisoner in Breen's car. then Breen consulted with Hitchcock and Walker a short distance from their cars.

"Turn off the radios in your cars so the suspects can't hear anything," Breen ordered. He switched to F2 on his portable radio, pressed the button, and said, "Four Twenty to Records, direct the responses on the last three subjects you were given to me."

Breen lit a cigarette and paced, waiting.

"Records to Four Twenty, ready to copy?"

"Go ahead."

"Got a confirmed NCIC hit on Cloward, Donald G. WMA, DOB 4-22-42. Parole violation, California Department of Corrections, no bail, will extradite. Confirmed second warrant. Armed robbery out of San Bernardino County, California, no bail."

After a pause of several seconds, Records continued. *"Confirmed NCIC hit on O'Donohue, Tyler D. WMA, DOB 7-7-43. Federal warrant for Unlawful Flight to Avoid Prosecution, Unlawful Possession of Controlled Substance With Intent To Sell, U.S. District Court in Boise, Idaho. Will extradite."*

Another pause.

"Confirmed King County Superior Court no-bail felony warrant for one count Extortion and one count Witness

Tampering on Askew, Thomas S. WMA, DOB 10-6-48. Will extradite."

DURING BOOKING, O'DONOHUE was discovered to have a large oval tattoo on his abdomen, the outside of which read 'Aryan Brotherhood' inside the upper ring. and a large red letter 'A' in the center. Askew had the initials "AB" tattooed on his left forearm and an ancient Irish symbol on his right shoulder.

The '64 Chevy Impala with California license plates they came in contained boxes of handgun and rifle ammunition, three black ski masks, and a map of Seattle with two locations in the Central District circled in red. LaPerle gave the map to Sergeant Breen. None would talk. Hitchcock and Walker booked them into the King County Jail.

Clearing the station just past midnight, they stopped at Sambo's before returning to their districts.

"Those guys are hard-core. All were armed, and two had priors for robbery," Hitchcock said.

"They probably just stopped for a drink after driving so long. Whatever they're here for, it ain't good."

"They sure were tatted out."

Walker nodded. "My dad told me about the Aryan Brotherhood, a white supremacist movement. Started in the California prisons so white inmates could protect themselves from the ethnic gangs. It's catching on in other states."

"What's their gig? Robbery?"

"And murder-for-hire."

Hitchcock took the last bite of his meal. "I'm heading back to The Wagon Wheel to talk to the employees, help them close. You coming?"

"Oh, yeah. The way that barmaid and you look at each other, I'd say you need a chaperone."

"Her name is Gayle."

"Uh-huh. Gayle-The-Fox."

THE LAST CUSTOMER to leave gave up trying to nag Ralph into giving him one more drink for the road left when Hitchcock and Walker returned.

"Who were those guys?" Ralph asked them.

"Ever heard of the Aryan Brotherhood?" Walker inquired.

A shocked expression came over Ralph's boyish features. "Yeah? Was that them? What were they doing here?"

"We asked the same question. They're ex-cons, so of course they wouldn't talk."

"They won't come back, will they?"

"They won't, and Hitchcock won't mention in his report who tipped him off, will you, Roger?"

Hitchcock didn't answer.

"Hey, Roger! We're over here!" Walker said, chuckling at the sight of Hitchcock and Gayle standing close together in the far corner.

"I had my gun with me," Ralph confided. "When I saw the one guy's gun, I asked myself if I could shoot if they tried to rob us."

"Well? How did you answer yourself?"

"I *probably* could, I guess," Ralph said after some hesitation.

Walker, in his usual playful mood, said, "Well, Ralph, 'probably' works for me!"

Still nervous, Ralph said, "Officer, you had your gun pressed against one guy's head tonight. You even cocked the hammer, which scared me and some customers. Could you have pulled the trigger?"

"Do bears crap in the woods?"

"Uhh, yeah, they do."

"That's my answer."

"Huh?"

"If he went for his weapon, you bet," Walker said. "Those guys give no mercy and ask none. You'd do well to remember that. And don't tell us about your gun in here anymore. You're legally not supposed to have one in a bar unless you're a cop, but *we* understand. I'll stick around to help you close."

"What about your partner?"

Walker looked at Hitchcock, in a corner talking with Gayle. "Roger? Looks like he's got another detail to take care of."

"Detail?"

Walker smiled patiently and shook his head. "Roger and Gayle got a birds-and-the-bees thing going, Ralph. Let's close this place up."

Ralph gave Walker a quizzical look. "Birds and bee thing?"

Walker chuckled and shook his head again. "Maybe I oughta check *your* ID, Ralph!"

† † †

AT THE STATION, Sergeant Breen wrote a memo to Detective Sergeant Jurgens:

> *Stan,*
>
> *We arrested three members of the Aryan Brotherhood for carrying concealed guns in The Wagon Wheel lounge. They were all wanted on felony warrants.*
>
> *A map of Seattle in their car had two locations in the Central District highlighted. We may have inadvertently prevented a hit.*
>
> *SPD should be alerted ASAP. Map is attached.*
>
> *Jack.*

CHAPTER THIRTY-SIX
The Longest Shadow

EVEN IN HIS late fifties, Doc Henderson's smile revealed the mischievous little boy he had been all his life. When his wife gave him a cake to deliver to Hitchcock, he knew it was time.

"Here, Doc. Take this to Roger while it's still warm."

"What if he doesn't like fruit cake?"

"He does. Trust me."

Doc shot a quizzical glance at his wife. "*How* do you know, Ethel, or should I ask?"

"I asked Myrna, of course. Why shouldn't I? We've been friends for twenty-five years."

"I thought so. I'll take it to him so you don't pump the lad for information on who he's dating now."

"I wouldn't do something so out of place, but *if* I did, my own curiosity would be my motive. I told Myrna she should ask him herself if she's so curious."

Doc sighed and shook his balding head as he

headed out the kitchen door.

"Be sure to invite him over for dinner one of these nights, and to bring a guest!" Ethel reminded Doc as he ambled across the patio, shaking his head ruefully.

Hitchcock was on his couch, playing his guitar when Doc knocked on the sliding glass door.

"The 'war department' wants to make sure you get this fresh out of the oven."

"Thanks, Doc," he said as he lifted the wax paper cover. "Fruitcake! How did Ethel know it's my favorite?"

Doc smiled and shook his head amusedly. *Don't you have a lot to learn. What you need is a wife.* "When can you come over for a little Yuletide cheer, meaning real whiskey, of course?"

"I've got tonight off, comp time. Got an early dinner date first."

"How about after seven tonight...say seven-thirty?"

"See you then."

HE TOOK ALLIE and Trevor for photos on Santa's lap at Frederick & Nelson in Bel Square, followed by dinner in the store's Rhododendron Room. He kissed Allie good night and headed home, sensing something important was up.

"This is the time," Doc said as he opened the kitchen door for him. He sat down in a deep leather chair before the crackling fire in Doc's living room, surrounded by framed mural scenes of mounted English hunters with packs of hounds around them. Doc poured golden liquid into tumblers.

"The best Irish whiskey, aged just right. Now, I'm not a religious man, Roger, but I do know what *sin* is," Doc said, flashing his boyish grin.

"And what would that be, Doc?" A question Hitchcock knew he was expected to ask.

"Sin is polluting whiskey like this with anything. It's too pure to be adulterated with water or even ice," Doc proclaimed, raspy relish in his voice. The warm glow of firelight enhanced the eternal boyishness of his features.

"I'll be the judge of that," Hitchcock said, smiling.

Doc handed a glass to him and hoisted his into the air for a toast. "To stout lads, and lassies with soft bodies and long hair," Doc proclaimed in a rumbling voice.

"Here, here," Hitchcock confirmed, clinking his glass against Doc's. They took their first sips together.

"Ahh. Smooth as silk. Ethel's gone to bed early. Her asthma is bothering her again. So, we can talk freely as men do," Doc said with an impish grin.

The fiery liquid warmed Hitchcock's throat all the way to his stomach and radiated glowing warmth throughout his body. He felt at home in Doc and Ethel's place. Except for the absence of a barn and horses, its size, style and decor reminded him of his childhood home. He savored the whiskey again as he stared into the magnificent fire, waiting for Doc to begin.

"I've wanted to tell you certain things about your dad ever since you moved in," Doc finally said. "He was the brother I never had, and I was the same to him. Because of him I returned here with Ethel after the War and built my practice after veterinary school. We grew up together. Neighbors, classmates. Like blood brothers, during the Depression." Doc paused, staring at the fire like he was enjoying an old family movie.

"Our families were neighbors, as I said. When my dad abandoned my mother and me, Ian, your grandfather, took me under his wing like a son. I often went home with your dad after school, and ate many dinners at your grandparents' place. After dinner, your grandparents helped us with our homework. This is the kind of people you come from, Roger.

"To this day, your father is on record as the best athlete in the history of Kirkland High School. Tall, strong, quick reflexes and well-coordinated, he had it all. We played football and baseball together, but your dad's talents shone best as a boxer, a trait he inherited from his dad. Every night before dinner, Ian drilled Ted in the fundamentals of punching, blocking, and footwork.

"I helped your dad by being his sparring partner until his training shifted to the gym in Seattle. After high school, Ted went to the UW on a scholarship to become a medical doctor like his dad. I went across the state to Washington State to become a veterinarian. Not everyone had phone service then, so we stayed in touch by letter."

Doc paused again, immersed in times past. Hitchcock held a reverential silence, absorbing every word Doc said.

"During the worst of the Depression, while Ted was a sophomore at the UW. your grandparents suffered a financial setback. Many of their patients lost their jobs and couldn't pay. Your grandfather continued caring for them at his expense, leaving it to them to pay if and when they could."

Hitchcock stirred in his seat, taking his eyes off Doc to focus on the flames. "Dad didn't tell me much about his college years."

"Your dad stepped up to the plate by trying his hand in the ring as a semi-pro. I was his corner man. In his first tryout he knocked out his opponent in the second round. When he knocked down his next opponent three times in the first round, he was admitted to the Washington Boxing Commission."

"Dad never told me much about his early fighting days either," Hitchcock said.

"Ted didn't like talking about himself. Anyway, he fought three-round exhibition fights every Friday at an arena on Capitol Hill which is long gone now. He gave the money to his parents, kept none for himself."

A rush of emotion swept over Hitchcock. "So, Dad was following what Granddad taught him?"

Doc didn't answer. He fell into silent reminiscing again. The soft glow of the firelight on his features seemed to turn back the years, and for a moment Hitchcock saw what Doc looked like as a young man. He lifted his gaze from the fire and cleared his throat.

"After your grandparents got their finances caught up with your dad's help," Doc continued as he straightened up in his chair, "your dad continued boxing, giving his prize money to needy families. Many of them were the black families of buddies he boxed with."

"I never knew this," Hitchcock said.

Doc chuckled. "Yeah, Ted was a private and modest man. I'm the only one he told this to. He felt strongly that colored people had been misjudged and mistreated in this country and this was his way of doing what he could to right the wrongs done to them."

"I knew Dad had empathy for black people but he never shared his views."

"No, he wouldn't. Whenever I came home from college, which wasn't often, I always attended his fights. I don't know of a single one he lost, though there must have been a few. He boxed and trained while carrying a full load in school and still got straight A's."

AS THE FIRE dimmed, Doc ambled over to the wood box and threw two small logs the size of fence posts onto the glowing coals. When the flames leaped to life again, he threw on two larger hunks of seasoned fir, which popped and crackled as the flames licked up the flue.

"I should have put alder on instead," he muttered reflectively. "Burns without the noise fir makes."

"This is perfect, Doc."

Doc poured more whiskey, first for Hitchcock, then himself. "We'll need more of this tonight, we've got more years to go, yet," he confided in his rumbling, lived-in voice. Hitchcock waited as Doc sat down, took a cigar from his humidor and savored the smoke before continuing.

"During this time, Ted wrote to me about a girl he met who was, he said, *the right one*—your mother. I was just ahead of him in that department. I proposed to Ethel right after meeting her at a school dance in Pullman.

"Then came the attack on Pearl Harbor, and everything changed. I joined the Navy and became a Hospital Corpsman, serving with the Marines in the Pacific, and your dad joined the Army, turning down an officer's commission to be an enlisted man, a medic. He went ashore with the infantry on the D-Day landing at Omaha Beach and several battles in Europe afterward. He never talked about it, but no doubt he saved many lives."

"He was decorated for bravery at D-Day," Hitchcock offered.

Doc nodded like he already knew this. He sipped his whiskey, relishing its warmth as it went down the pipe. He relit his cigar, and through a wreath of smoke, he continued. "During the war, we mailed our letters to each other's parents, to be forwarded to us if possible. After we came home, we finished our degrees, double-dated a few times and married our gals. We took turns being best men at our weddings and became god-parents to each other's kids. I'll bet you didn't know that did you?"

Hitchcock shook his head, too amazed to speak.

"Your dad was one of the last—and best—of a vanishing breed of physician. At a time when family medicine became less personal, your dad continued to make house calls, to respond to family emergencies in the middle of the night, to help the police and fire departments and ordinary citizens, even if they couldn't pay."

His voice thickened by emotion, Hitchcock offered, "I remember the times Dad took me with him on calls to help the police or the fire department when someone was injured. Watching him care for people inspired me."

"I didn't know that, Roger, but your dad taking you along with him explains who you are now."

"I also remember being fascinated by the officers' uniforms and gun belts."

"Whether you realize it or not, Roger, you are following in his footsteps."

"How so?"

"You're not a doctor, but helping and protecting is your code as much as it was his. Under the long shadow of his father Ian's influence and guidance, your father learned discipline and how to handle adversity through boxing and wartime military service. Under the shadow of your father's influence, you learned discipline, to thrive in adversity through boxing and wartime military service. Ted's gone. You are your own man now, but his shadow remains over you, and it's a long, loving shadow. It has guided you and will continue to guide you. So, now is the time…"

Doc opened the drawer of the table next to his chair and withdrew a packet of envelopes tied together with string. He held the packet in his hands and looked at Hitchcock.

"Grief haunted me long after your father passed. I've never been a believer in a personal God, but knowing your dad and your grandfather inclines me in that direction to this day They were devout Christian men."

"I knew Dad was. He got into a strange movement in Seattle before he died."

Doc held up the packet of envelopes. "I remember. Father Dennis Bennett, leader of some sort of a charismatic movement in an Episcopal church in Seattle. Ted became very excited about it and tried to convert me."

"What was your response?"

"I told your dad that Jesus was a great teacher, but not the Son of God," Doc said, shaking his head doubtfully.

"How could someone falsely claim to be the Son of God be a great teacher?" Hitchcock said, surprised at himself.

Doc fell silent, seeming to search his mind for an answer. "But I digress," he finally muttered, avoiding the subject. "I came home to find your dad's letters here and unopened. After you were born, Ted asked if I still had them. When I said yes, he asked me to give them to you when I saw fit. I remember being puzzled at the time, but I agreed. He probably sensed he would die early."

He handed the bundle to Hitchcock.

"I'm at a loss for words, Doc."

"Words aren't always enough."

"Does Ethel know about this?"

Still holding his glowing cigar, Doc chuckled and shook his head.

"What's so funny?"

"I thought your dad taught you *something* about women!"

The evening of fireside revelation and superb whiskey ended. Hitchcock stayed up until he finished reading each of his father's letters.

He felt a shift coming as he put them in his safe.

CHAPTER THIRTY-SEVEN
A Matter of Knowing

DIFFUSED SUNLIGHT BRIGHTENED the surrounding greenery as Hitchcock knelt in front of his father's headstone. He felt grateful for the respect the grounds-keeper, one of his father's patients, gave his gravesite.

"Last night, Doc Henderson gave me the letters you wrote to him during the war, Dad. I read them all. I know things about you now that even Mom never knew. Now I understand that under your shadow I studied in school, worked summers, went to medical school, and when I quit school to join the Army, I was pursuing you—and your shadow was over me."

He paused. "After I left here last time, I took some time off, worked at a ranch for a week, and came back knowing police work is my calling. Reading your letters confirmed it, but I miss you, Dad, especially our talks."

He drove to the Pancake Corral. As he walked through

the double doors, in his mind's eye he remembered as a five-year old standing next to his dad as he joked with Bill Chace. It suddenly came to him that *his dad* always ordered buckwheats, bacon and coffee.

When Allie greeted him as if she knew he would come, he wondered if it was a mystical pull that brought him to this place. *Is it habit, or Allie, or maybe my dad?* He said nothing as Allie seated him in her section and poured coffee without a word.

"I've got something to ask you," she said.

"Your wish is my command."

"Good! I'll hold you to it. Tomorrow at three I'm singing Christmas songs for the shut-ins at Swedish Hospital. Our guitar player is down with the flu, so since you play guitar, you can fill in. I hope you can sing, too."

"Hold on a second. What if I'm already committed to something else?"

She smiled. "You're not, and besides, Roger Hitchcock, you said my wish is your command."

"We should have at least one practice session first."

"My mom will be at my place at two-thirty. Come at one or one-thirty, we'll practice then."

"Your place at one. Now can I have a menu?"

"You don't need a menu. You know it by heart."

"Yes, but I use it to hide behind while I watch you work," he teased.

"You use the newspaper for that. What'll you have?"

He handed the menu back without looking at it, happy in the knowledge that she had been eyeing him too all this time.

"Buckwheats and bacon, what else?"

CHAPTER THIRTY-EIGHT
A Yuletide Romance

AT ONE O'CLOCK sharp, Hitchcock knocked on Allie's door, guitar case in hand, hoping for a kiss. His heart skipped a beat at the sight of her in a powder-blue cashmere sweater dress which spoke volumes of her physical perfection.

Golden hair tied back in a ponytail, no jewelry or makeup, which he didn't think she needed. Her smile when he saw her rendered him helpless.

"Shhh," she whispered. "Trevor just fell asleep. I have coffee and bran muffins for us."

She slipped her arm over his neck, stood on her tip-toes. Their lips locked. He encircled her waist in his arms and prolonged the kiss until she pulled him inside and closed the door. He sat on the couch, and took his guitar from its case as she set two cups and a plate on the coffee table.

"Thanks for coming. This means a lot to me. Would

you play something?"

He tuned his strings, then started playing. "Do you recognize this old tune?"

She shook her head. "Sorta familiar, but…"

"*Red River Valley*. How about this one?"

She laughed. "Nope. But it sounds familiar, too."

"*On Top of Old Smokey*."

"You play folk songs. Nice. Can you read music?"

He nodded.

"Here's sheet music for a few Christmas carols."

He leaned toward her on the couch, almost laying on her lap, playfully acting like he wanted to read the music, then lifted his lips with a twinkle in his eyes, looking for another kiss.

She broke into laughter as she gently pushed him back. "Silly boy!"

He leaned toward her again, playful hunger in his eyes. Blushing, Allie kissed him, worried he might hear her heart racing. He kissed her back, holding it until she put her hand on his shoulder and pulled back.

"My mom will be here any time," she said breathlessly just as a knock at the door came.

Agnes did a double-take when she saw the blush on her daughter's face.

"Hi, Mom. Thanks for coming. Roger was just practicing with his guitar. The regular guitar player from the church can't make it today so Roger agreed to help me play and sing carols at the hospital this afternoon."

Agnes gave a 'who-do-you-think-you're-kidding' look at her daughter as she took off her coat. "Practicing, eh? How come I didn't hear any music when I stood at the door?"

Allie gazed at the floor with a sheepish grin and said nothing. She didn't see her mother wink and smile at Hitchcock.

"Trevor's asleep?"

Allie nodded.

"You two better get going. I'll feed him when he wakes."

† † †

MEMORIES OF PHU Loi came over Hitchcock as he walked with Allie down the sterile corridor of the sixth floor to the nurse administrator's office. The overriding smell of antiseptic reminded him of rows of wounded soldiers waiting to be flown to the big hospital at Long Binh.

The receptionist recognized Allie and handed them visitor badges. No one else from Allie's church showed up.

The patients in the first room were two men in their fifties or sixties. IV tubes ran into the arms of both. The one closest to the door was asleep. The one by the window waved them in, smiling.

Allie sang *Silent Night* in soprano, surprising him with her clarity and vibrato. She knew all four stanzas by heart, ending on a long note. One of the patients gazed out the window past the steel gray skies, perhaps into a warmer past as his eyes filled with tears.

They went room to room, singing to lonely souls until they reached a children's room where, seeing a nine-year-old girl, bald from cancer treatments, her parents in the room with her, overwhelmed Hitchcock with grief and compassion. Allie motioned for him to join her in singing "Joy to the World." He was surprised at how well his voice harmonized with hers and how the lyrics penetrated him. He stopped mid-song. Tears that came when the girl's parents joined in the singing choked him up.

Allie became even more beautiful to him now, as if he had never known any woman but her. "I want to do this again with you," he told her over dinner at Nick's afterward.

Her heart overflowing with warmth, Allie reached across the table for his hand. "Yes, I want you to," she replied.

"It's a date, then," he said, taking her hand.

CHAPTER THIRTY-NINE
Two Stalkers and
The Stranger

DEMONS CLAWED THE insides of the older sexual predator, the first of his type to stalk the women of the city. So strong were his urgings that he struggled to keep from writhing in his seat during his return flight from Las Vegas to Seattle. For relief he paid the cab driver extra to wait while he made a brief visit to a certain massage parlor near the airport.

He thought about his wife as the cab took him the rest of the way home. Meek little Mona wasn't so little anymore. She had packed on the pounds to the point he wouldn't be seen with her in public or at company parties. Her pleading for marriage counseling disgusted him, but as his squeaky-clean wife, she gave him the cloak of respectability he needed.

As the married, prosperous, upstanding member of

the business community, no one would suspect him for the terror he was becoming. For that reason, he would always keep Mona. She went along with whatever he did without question, as long as he provided for her creature comforts, she kept a clean home and respected his privacy, and he could carry out the fantasies that were accelerating his decline.

True, he had returned for his business, but his real reason was to hunt anew in his personal hunting ground, Bellevue's blue-collar neighborhoods. It had been almost two months since a composite sketch of him had been in the local papers. He had stayed out of town long enough for the public memory of the sketch to fade and the facial injuries he received from the young cop he barely escaped from, the former boxer he read about in the paper, to heal.

He walked up the driveway to his front door, again feeling the thrill of stalking, dominating, terrorizing, taking control.

The house was empty. The half-eaten box of cookies on the kitchen counter disgusted him. *Has she no pride in herself?* He considered it a personal insult that his trophy wife had let herself go so badly.

He ignored the stacks of mail on his desk. His heart raced as he dialed the combination of his safe. He took out a large manila envelope. Sordid fantasies made him oblivious to his surroundings as his soul feasted on dark pornographic images. He fondled trophies from past conquests: women's under-wear, a hairbrush, and clumps of hair he took from his victims to remember them by; souvenirs of his escapades. He smirked, knowing that by themselves they couldn't incriminate him.

Stripped to the waist, he inspected himself in the full-length mirror in the master closet. At fifty-seven, every muscle, vein and tendon stood out under a layer of paper-thin skin. His body could pass as a thirty-year-old athlete. Only his full head of silver hair hinted otherwise.

He slipped on a green T-shirt and a black windbreaker over that. His blue-hooded sweatshirt he left in its hiding place under the stack of folded sweaters in the bottom drawer of his dresser.

His special-ordered gray Dodge Aspen with Oregon license plates started at the first turn of the key. The motor throbbed as he backed out of the garage.

After cruising neighborhoods on the east side of the city for a half-hour, something drew him to a certain lower middle-class neighborhood in Lake Hills. The crisp air and lack of rain had the "little people" as he called them, walking the streets, their little ones in tow, dogs on leashes, doing yard work, washing their cars in their driveways.

Young working-class women were his preferred victims. He found them more attractive than women of aristocratic families such as his. The only working-class people he saw during his childhood were live-in maids, usually East European immigrants his father exploited. Like his father, he had found young, blue-collar girls to have a no-frills, earthy understanding of what their bodies were about; sex, child-bearing, and hard work, all of which they approached matter-of-factly, without shame, false modesty or embarrassment.

He thought of himself as royalty taking his rightful privileges with the peasant women of his domain. The victims who yielded to his demands did so as if they were paying homage to the lord of the manor, which reinforced his elitist views of himself.

Wearing a tan ball cap to hide his silver hair from notice, he parked against the curb in a neighborhood of poorly maintained, one-story and split-level homes.

The thrill of being back on the stalk almost overpowered him as he stepped out of his car. Lust surged through him as he made a show of stretching beside his car, leaning against it, and bending from the waist to reach his toes, as runners do.

He began to jog.

A pretty, slender brunette, early twenties, the blue-collar type he preferred, arrived in the driveway of a run-down split-level house in an older forest-green VW Beetle. Her ring finger was bare as she got her baby out of her car and went through the front door. He glimpsed her going downstairs as the door closed.

He would return later to scout the house. For now

he explored the streets to plan two escape routes, one for a normal departure, the other if the police were too close. He smiled as he drove, imagining the future fear on his next victim's face, followed by surrender.

† † †

HIDING UNDER THE bed in Room 4 of the Bellevue Motel, a collection of white, wood-sided, green-roofed ramshackle '40s vintage cottages on the road between Bellevue's downtown and the town of Kirkland, a young man waited. He heard the man in the bed above snoring, but not the woman.

The gold Rolex his parents gave him for his twenty-first birthday read 3:50 a.m. *All the cops are at the station, changing shift.* He heard no noise other than the man's snoring. Assuming the woman slept quietly, he slid out from under the bed without making a sound. He knew from listening to them that they first met in a bar last night. He scribbled a note on motel notepaper and placed it on the dresser:

> *Thanks for the show last night.*
> *You get an A-minus.*
> *Please come back again soon.*

As a going-away prank, he took their clothes and car keys and urinated on them in the brushy field behind the motel. He hid further back in the bushes, waiting to watch the police arrive. But this time, as he waited, he realized that peeping didn't thrill him like it once did.

† † †

THE MIDDLE-AGE MAN roaming around Wilburton Hill in an old pickup came across perfectly as what he wasn't–an aging country boy from Kansas or thereabouts. His round, clean-shaven, ruddy face was boyish and friendly. His reddish hair was cut short and traditional. He wore frayed, plaid flannel shirts, loose-fitting blue jeans, threadbare at the knees, frayed at the cuffs, and scuffed brown leather work boots.

His bland, joe-average appearance was adopted to make him unnoticeable to college-educated, well-paid crowd who tended to ignore blue-collar people. He developed a mild Midwest drawl and learned to flash a broad, winning, innocent smile to deepen his deception.

No one, not even those who hired him, knew his true history, which, though extensive, wasn't public property.

The stranger charged high fees for his work. Just as nondescript as his Midwest country boy act was his vehicle of choice for this job, a tan, early '60s Ford F100 half-ton pickup, straight-six-cylinder under the hood, stick shift on the floor.

He spent days poking around Wilburton Hill, directly above City Hall and the police station, on foot and in his truck in which he sometimes placed a lawn mower in the bed to explain himself and ease fears without saying a word.

Only once did the stranger drive all the way down the long gravel road to the Henderson place. After discovering that the road ended there, that there was no place to turn around or park without going up into the Henderson's driveway, he looked for another way to access the property.

Cruising the surrounding area, careful not to attract attention, the stranger discovered an old logging road which led through dense forest from Hyak Junior High to the back of the cabana at the Henderson place. Thereafter, the stranger parked at the school and walked the trail to the cabana at different times of day and night.

He spent much time at the public library across the parking lot from the police station. Pretending to be reading, he watched officers changing shifts without attracting attention.

When he ate at the Pancake Corral, which he did almost daily, he asked to be seated at the smaller tables at the front, where he listened to conversations as the cooks worked, waitresses picked up their orders, and customers paid. No one noticed the stranger watching Allie when she was there. He was too well-trained and experienced for that.

A new 7-11 store opened, kitty-corner from the Pancake Corral. Because he liked to smoke after a meal, the stranger often went there to buy cigarettes.

CHAPTER FORTY
In the Name of Evil

IN A HOUSE in the Fremont district of Seattle, Bruce Sands, alias 'Jim Reynolds' picked up his phone on the second ring.

"When was your last contact with the little waitress?" Olson asked.

"Weeks ago. I just got out of jail, Mister –"

"Stop! No names. Our phones could be tapped. You risked our whole operation by being sloppy and getting thrown in jail. You can't afford to be stupid or careless. What's the status of your parole now?"

"My parole officer accepted my explanation. I'm still in good standing."

"Then we'll proceed, but if you get into any more trouble, you're through. Understand?"

"Yes, sir."

"All right. My clients want you to meet her again as soon as possible. I'm sure you need money after just getting out of jail."

"Money first. You still owe me from last time."

"I'll meet you tomorrow with the cash I owe you and an advance for your next contact," Olson said. "We'll meet at the same café in the lower level of the Pike Place Market. Set up a meeting with the waitress, then report to me when and where you'll be seeing her so I can be there ahead of time."

"Tomorrow, then. Noon?"

"Yes. One more thing. She's dating a Bellevue cop now. The one who gunned down a drug dealer last month. His name is Hitchcock. I'll give you a photo of him so you'll know him on sight. Be careful."

"Don't worry. I'll know how to deal with him," he said.

"I figured you would. Noon tomorrow. Be on time."

OLSON GAVE SANDS cash and a news photograph of Hitchcock when they met in the lower level of the Pike Place Market above the Seattle waterfront. "The officer on the right is dating Allison, or Allie, as she likes to be called. Besides killing a drug dealer last month, Hitchcock is a combat veteran and a former boxer, so be careful," Olson added.

Sands smirked as he stared at the photograph of Hitchcock. "No sweat. I studied cop tactics in prison."

Sands called Allie's phone number. He panicked when the recording said the number is disconnected.

The ample income stream from Olson would dry up if he couldn't find her.

He grabbed his .357 Magnum and a box of .38 Special practice ammunition and headed east on Highway 10, taking the Bellevue exit. His anxiety increased when he didn't see Allie's Toyota at the Pancake Corral. He found it in the Bay Vue parking lot. He tucked his revolver into the back of his waistband, covered it with his jacket and knocked on the door of her apartment. He was surprised when an older woman answered.

"Is Allie here?" Sands asked, making his best effort to smile and seem friendly.

Taken aback by his sinister presence and forced smile, Agnes sharply replied, "No."

"I tried calling but her number's disconnected. Will she be back soon?"

"I'm her mother. Who are you?" Agnes snapped.

He hesitated, trying to remember which alias he gave Allie. "Uh, Jim Reynolds. Allie knows me. Would you ask her to call me when she gets back? She has my number."

"I will," Agnes replied as she shut the door.

Sands scowled as he returned to his Volvo. He didn't know what to make of Allie's disconnected phone, her car being at her apartment but she's not there. Or was she actually inside? No. Her mother was there as the babysitter.

Taking Highway 10 east to the Preston exit, Sands drove to a secluded grove of trees by the Raging River. He switched to practice ammunition and shot large fir trees at different ranges, while on the move, standing, kneeling and crouched behind the fender of his Volvo, imagining the trees to be uniformed police officers.

With his last six rounds of practice ammunition, he backed his car toward a large fir tree until it was at his left rear quarter panel. He laid the revolver on the armrest of the driver door, barrel pointed back at the tree, where an officer would be standing and practiced opening the door about six inches and pulling the trigger, hitting the tree.

He imagined scenes of killing policemen as he reloaded hollow-point "cop killer" ammunition in case a cop stopped him on his way back to Seattle.

† † †

NIGHT HAD FALLEN when Hitchcock brought Allie back to her apartment. He kissed her at the door and headed home to change into his uniform. His phone rang as he arrived. Allie sounded nervous.

"Roger, my mom says Jim Reynolds came by while we were out. I'm scared because he shouldn't know where I live. He wants me to call him. What should I do?"

He thought for a moment. "Call him back, ask him what he wants. If he wants another meeting, tell him you won't have time until after the holidays. Don't give him your new number. Call me back after you've talked to him."

Five minutes later Allie called. "He agreed to wait," she said.

"Good. Now we go to the next step."

"Next step?"

"We've changed your phone number, now you're going to move. I know of a couple places which are quieter, safer and more convenient. I'll make the arrangements."

"Am I in danger, Roger?"

"I can't say no. As I showed you, his real name is Bruce Sands and his rap sheet includes federal armed robbery and weapons charges."

"You showed me his prison photograph. Trevor and I aren't safe, are we?"

"Start packing."

CHAPTER FORTY-ONE
Winding Down, Gearing Up

THE RADIO HAD been quiet for hours until someone finally keyed their mic. *"T'was the night before Christmas, and all through the town, not a creature was stirring, not even our mayor, our clown,"* someone who sounded like Walker sang on the air. The radio crackled as others keyed their mics to transmit jokes and laughter.

The bars closed by 1:00 a.m. Streets were almost empty. Someone who sounded like Ray Packard keyed his mic with Santa Claus impersonations. *"Ho-ho-ho, Merry Christmas! What did you want for Christmas that I didn't get you, officer?"*

A voice disguised as a little boy, probably Otis, came on the air. *"A new Chief, Santa! I asked for a new Chief!"* *Another voice that sounded like Walker said "Santa, I want a new wife, and a rich girlfriend,"* and on it went.

Hitchcock listened to the comedy and laughed as he patrolled and re-patrolled his beat.

COMEDY HOUR ON police radio aside, it was *too* quiet. Hitchcock and Walker prowled their beats, leaving no stone unturned, finding nothing. They met at the town dump below the freeway and the frontage road. They rolled their windows down, turned their radios up and climbed over the cyclone fence. Hitchcock killed two rats and Walker one by the time Dispatch sent them on the usual citizen "shots fired" calls. They reloaded with duty ammo, climbed the fence, answered their radios, and met at Sambo's for coffee.

OTIS WASN'T ONE to go to coffee with the guys when it got quiet as it did now. Everything in Crossroads had closed at 10:00 p.m. Mall parking lots had emptied out. Traffic dwindled to a trickle. Though the weather was cold and drizzling, Otis shifted to foot patrol. He called out, leaving his cruiser parked behind the Crossroads Mall.

An experienced woodsman and hunter, he knew that all environments are sensitive to intrusion. For several minutes he stood in the shadows like a tree in a dark forest, hunting with his ears and eyes, taking stock of his surroundings with only his eyes moving until the immediate environment accepted his presence and resettled.

As he hunted deer and elk in dark forests, he took one or two steps, stopped where there was cover, a building, a fence, or a vehicle, or a shadow to break up his outline, and waited, motionless. He moved in an irregular pattern, using long pauses to give the environment time to absorb his presence. Thus he moved, able to hear and see as a good burglar or a prowler would, things he would miss sitting in a car.

In this way Otis checked closed businesses front and back, and parked cars. At a one-story dental office he discovered the stone-cold body of a young white male lying on his left side in the middle of the parking lot, his arms and legs wrapped around a long metal gas canister. An outdoor wood enclosure next to the dental office was open, the broken padlock on the pavement. Three similar gas cannisters were inside, a fourth was missing.

The valve on the cannister between the dead man's legs was open. Otis observed lividity in the man's face, neck and hands. Given the cold, he estimated death occurred three hours ago. He recognized the victim from previous arrests; drug-related every time. He began the long walk back for the radio in his cruiser.

AT 2:00 A.M. in the downtown, four drunk car salesmen staggered out of the ritzy Crabapple restaurant in Bellevue Square, where the city's most well-to-do dined and drank. One fell into the wishing well outside the front doors, causing two others to nearly drown trying to rescue him. Their loud laughter and cursing drew

Brooks from his regular rounds to the scene. He called two cabs after relieving them of their keys so they couldn't return and drive away after he left. He tossed the keys into the dealership night drop and resumed patrol.

FRENCHIE LAPERLE SAT sipping a large cup of coffee from the 7-11 on Main at 104th. The night air was dry and cold, traffic almost nil. LaPerle had his window down. Suddenly movement across the intersection caught his eye. He stared for a few seconds, then shook his head. "I must be tired, I'm seeing things," he told himself.

His eye caught movement again. It came from the Christmas tree lot across the intersection on the southeast corner. Puzzled, he focused his binoculars on the trees. Sure enough, one tree in the middle kept wiggling.

LaPerle said, "What the–?"

At the third shaking, he keyed his mic and called Dispatch.

Almost a minute passed before Radio answered. *Wayne and Shirley are either scarfing down dessert or messing around again in the radio room,* LaPerle figured.

The huskiness in Wayne's voice suggested something other than Christmas cookies was going on. *Radio to Three Zero Three–go.*

"I hate to interrupt your holiday fun, but I'll be out of the car investigating a Christmas tree doing the hootchee-kootchee at 104th and Main, southeast corner."

10-4, Three Zero Three checking out a wiggling tree, Dispatch replied, laughter in the background.

He crossed the intersection, thinking he had a couple frisky teenagers in the act of mutually plucking forbidden fruit. He exited his cruiser, aiming his flashlight into the grove of cut evergreen trees.

"All right! Come on out, you two! I know you're in there," he ordered.

No answer. One tree in the center continued wiggling.

"If I have to come in there to get you, I'll charge you with trespassing. Come out!"

Still no answer. LaPerle moved in, flashlight hand, pushing aside the green branches of other trees, gun hand kept free, just in case. He came to the source of the shaking, a large black Lab, his leash caught around the base of a tree. Every time LaPerle called, the dog wagged its tail and tried to come to him, shaking the tree.

When LaPerle finally stopped laughing, he untangled the leash and stroked the dog's head and neck. "Well, big fella, am I glad to find you and not a bad guy! Let's find out where you live." He happily keyed his mic: "Three Zero Three, Radio, I'm headed to the station with one in custody. Advise Four Twenty I'll need help with this one!"

A MILE NORTH of Bellevue's downtown core along

104th Avenue, was the Bellevue Motel. Like its cousin motels in Eastgate, it was built in the late '40s, a collage of small, red brick one-room cottages which could be rented by the hour most nights. After the bars closed at two a.m., rooms rented by the hour sold briskly, especially on Friday nights.

Shortly after two a.m. a smirking man and a gushing woman, both reeking of alcohol, paid cash for a room. After eager physical intimacy, the man fell asleep. The woman went into the bathroom to wash. A loud burp erupted from the bedroom.

"Richie! Shame on you," she giggled from the bathroom. No reply. She came around the corner to the bedroom. Not only was Richie still passed out, she was horrified when another man, in his early twenties, crawled out from under the bed.

The woman cowered in the farthest corner and crossed her arms over her private parts. "Don't you hurt me! Don't you dare hurt me!"

The well-dressed young man wearing a gold Rolex watch smiled at her. "I wouldn't hurt you, lady. Thanks for the show, but I give you two only a C minus," he said as calmly as if reporting he had just fixed a leaking toilet.

He pocketed the two sets of car keys on the nightstand and took their clothes as he left. The woman screamed nonstop until the night manager came. "What's wrong, ma'am?" the wizened little old man asked.

"A strange man came out from hiding under our bed! He was there the whole time! Call the police!" she shouted, finally covering herself with a towel.

"Right away!" the manager said as he turned to leave for the office.

"No! Stop!" she shouted. "Whatever you do, *don't* call the cops!"

"Huh?"

"No, I said! Forget it. Do you understand?"

"Why?" he asked.

"Oh, *come on*! How could you be in this business and not understand?"

The night clerk glanced at the sleeping man in the bed, then at his wedding ring. The woman wore no wedding ring. They paid cash, he remembered, and neither signed the register. He nodded without smiling. "Yes, ma'am. No cops."

THE HOLIDAYS THIS year were a highwire act for Hitchcock. He had social obligations to meet while keeping his informants away from each other. One in particular had to kept out of the spotlight as he made the rounds of Christmas parties. He went alone to any party involving the City to avoid problems with Eve. To Gayle he took presents and treated her to an out-of-town dinner where they wouldn't be recognized.

He paid brief home visits to Randy Fowler and Will Hodges, but he took Allie to Christmas dinner at his mother's, where he introduced her to his family. On Christmas Day Allie took him to her mother's home in Renton, where she introduced him to her brothers and their wives.

A STRANGE ANXIETY dominated the squad's final six days of the year. Shift change was coming up, but that didn't account for it. The unsettled mood of the country over the economy and the war weren't the cause of it either. As the squad looked forward to rotating to day shift for the next three months, the days went by in a flash.

At the late afternoon threshold of New Year's Eve, Hitchcock already detected a sense of "one more round" in the air.

The Patrol Division did its best to be ready for a night of heavy calls. To meet the additional manpower needs, Hitchcock volunteered to come in on overtime. The entire Traffic Division, which normally didn't work past 10:00 p.m., would be out in force for all-night DWI emphasis patrols.

CHAPTER FORTY-TWO
The Last Shift

New Year's Eve
7:45 P.M.

ARGUING VOICES IN the booking room carried all the way down the hall to the squad room where Sergeant Breen faced his beefed-up squad of ten officers from the podium. Ignoring the racket, he read the latest bulletin of stolen cars, car prowls, strongarm robbery suspect descriptions, in-progress domestic violence incidents.

He looked at his men. "We're in for a heavy night," he said. "Second shift has been rolling from one call after another for the last two hours. As this is our last night shift before we rotate to days, let's back each other up tonight so no one gets hurt. Diss-*missed!*"

Hitchcock radioed himself in service as he rolled out of the station. He didn't mind working New Year's Eve, but after three months of high-octane nights, he thought of working the day shift as he would a long Hawaiian vacation.

THE BARS WERE hopping and calls were pouring in as he drove along the winding curves of tree-lined Richards Road toward Eastgate. He could hear live rock music through the walls and closed doors of The Steak Out as he entered the parking lot.

A couple in a yellow Ford Torino ducked down as Hitchcock drove by. He got out and shined his flashlight into the car. A young blonde woman in the front passenger seat sat up when he knocked on the window.

He heard the man next to her, shaggy dark hair, beard, wearing granny glasses, a crude imitation of John Lennon, tell her, "Don't open the window." Hitchcock jerked the door open before she pushed the lock button.

The stench of marijuana smoke and beer hit his nostrils. He spotted a packet of white powder on the passenger side floor, a baggie of marijuana and a pipe on the seat, and an open bottle of beer on the driver side floor. He arrested them both, impounded the car and took them in handcuffs to the station. Thus began Hitchcock's final shift of 1970.

TRAFFIC OFFICERS WERE dispatched to back up the squad as they raced from call to call—assisting the State Patrol on drunk driving arrests on the freeway, breaking up loud parties, disturbances in bars, and violent family beefs. The holding cells had to be emptied twice by two officers to take prisoners to jail in Seattle in order to make room for more prisoners. Several times an officer had to be pulled off a call to back up another officer on a family beef or a disturbance. It was New Year's Eve, with more hours to go.

THE PREDATOR WHO escaped from Hitchcock weeks ago parked a block from a certain starter home in Lake Hills. After his narrow escape from arrest, he changed his MO to wearing loose-fitting pants and a blue hooded sweatshirt as a disguise. He never imagined it would become such a trademark that someone else would copy it.

He walked lawn-to-lawn to make a quiet approach to a certain house. Seeing the young woman's VW Beetle in the driveway, he unlatched the gate to the back yard. Finding the sliding glass door unlocked, he slipped inside and crossed the room, his soft-soled sneakers not making a sound as he headed for the bedroom door.

IN THE FREMONT district of Seattle, Bruce Sands loaded a .357 Magnum revolver he had stolen in a burglary with hollow-point ammunition and tucked it into the back of his waistband. His looked with mild disdain at his former cellmates, the woman bank robber from Oregon and another man with her, all passed out from wine and cocaine, lying on decrepit furniture or the floor. He headed over the Evergreen Bridge to Bellevue in his decrepit grayish-green '59 Volvo. He patted his shirt pocket to make sure he had the photo of the officer he was after as he approached City Hall.

It was 3:40 a.m. He saw patrol cars entering the station parking lot.

It would be daylight in two hours.

ACKNOWLEDGEMENTS

The authenticity of The Bluesuit Chronicles would not be possible without the continued support of certain retired members of the Bellevue and Seattle Police Departments who have helped me with placing major events in correct historical order. Thanks to Deborah J Ledford for her editing and formatting of this the third, and revised edition. Many thanks also to Jessica Bell for her excellent cover design, and her patience with me regarding the finer details of this cover. Special thanks to fellow veteran, police officer and author, Elvis Bray, whose assistance on the earlier editions of this book were of great value to this the third printing.

ABOUT THE AUTHOR

JOHN HANSEN draws from personal experience for most of his writing. Between 1966-1970 he served as a Gunners Mate aboard an amphibious assault ship that ran solo missions in and out of the rivers and waterways of South Vietnam and other places.

While a patrol officer with the Bellevue Police Department, his fellow officers nicknamed him "Mad Dog" for his tenacity. After ten years in Patrol, he served eleven years as a detective, investigating homicide, suicide, robbery, assault, arson and rape cases.

As a private investigator since retirement, his cases have taken him across the United States and to other countries and continents. He is the winner of several awards for his books, short stories and essays.

Made in the USA
Columbia, SC
13 July 2021

41766393R00186